The vixen had come, right out ... *. . b...*
It was as if she had been looking right into him. As if she
... *th the turmoil inside his head . . . Suddenly, Kegan knew his*
... *ould never be the same again.*

gan's life could do with a change. Stuck with a bullying,
inken dad and a mum too worn down to care, the only
asure in his life is to go to the local scrapyard and draw
foxes he's discovered there. And when tragedy strikes,
;an's fight to save the foxes from the developers, with
help of his friend, Zoë, keeps him going and restores
..is faith in the future.

e Welford was born in Sussex and trained to be a
retary before giving up paid work to bring up her
ldren. When they started school, she had several part-
ne jobs, and then became an editorial writer with a local
wspaper. When she was made redundant, she continued
ting at home and had several articles published in
magazines. After five rejected novels, her first book for
oung adults was published in 1989. *Out of the Blue* is the
inth of her books to be published by Oxford University
'ress.

Out of the Blue

Other books by Sue Welford

Out of the Blue

Sue Welford

OXFORD
UNIVERSITY PRESS

OXFORD
UNIVERSITY PRESS

Great Clarendon Street, Oxford OX2 6DP

Oxford University Press is a department of the University of Oxford.
It furthers the University's objective of excellence in research, scholarship,
and education by publishing worldwide in

Oxford New York

Athens Auckland Bangkok Bogotá Buenos Aires Calcutta
Cape Town Chennai Dar es Salaam Delhi Florence Hong Kong Istanbul
Karachi Kuala Lumpur Madrid Melbourne Mexico City Mumbai
Nairobi Paris São Paulo Singapore Taipei Tokyo Toronto Warsaw

and associated companies in Berlin Ibadan

Oxford is a registered trade mark of Oxford University Press
in the UK and in certain other countries

British Library Cataloguing in Publication Data available

ISBN 0 19 271839 8

1 3 5 7 9 10 8 6 4 2

Typeset by AFS Image Setters Ltd, Glasgow

Printed and bound in Great Britain by
Biddles Ltd, Guildford and King's Lynn

A calm will descend and there's peace at the end
of the darkest night.

Sometimes I cry, sometimes I fly like a bird.

from 'Fly Like a Bird' by Boz Scaggs

It was the twilight of a cold winter's evening when Kegan first saw the vixen. She was close to the scrapyard gates. She had been standing by the wreck of an old Ford Escort, her nose tuned to the wind, her eyes scanning for danger. When she spotted him she stood stock still and stared. She had come, right out of the blue, to be there with him. It was as if she had been looking right into him. As if she could see all the turmoil inside his head.

Snowflakes had been drifting in the wind. She'd had some on her back, on her tail. They sparkled like diamonds in the fur of her coat. He loved all wild animals but this was the most beautiful one he had ever seen.

She had gazed at him for another fleeting moment then slunk silently away between two wrecked cars. He hadn't been able to move after that. It was as if his feet had grown roots. He had just stood there watching the empty space that she had filled with her elegance.

'She saw me!' He'd felt a ghost snake down his spine. *'She looked right inside me.'*

Suddenly, Kegan knew his life would never be the same again.

Later he had dreamed of her. Slink he had called her. He *was* her. Padding down alleyways, jumping noiselessly over walls, foraging in piles of garbage for scraps of food. Looking this way. That. Eyes forever warily scanning. Pouncing on mice, rats. Once a pigeon, too frozen with cold to perch high up. He felt the feathers tickling his nose as he plucked them from the bony breast with his sharp teeth. Behind the pub, he had felt the stinging smell of beer touch his nostrils, the

1

stink of rotting rubbish, the hard metallic smell of the scrapyard, the scent of her greatest enemy. Man. Magnified a million times he'd heard the echoing sound of the motorway traffic, the whine of planes overhead, the mechanical thud, thud of loud rock music from a café jukebox. His ears pricked to the squeak of bats, the chirp of roosting sparrows, the quick, dark breaths of the night. And when he woke up, shivering under his covers in the bitter winter's morning, he felt he had known what it was like to be free.

The scrapyard was Kegan's favourite place. He went there whenever he could. Mostly at weekends and after school. Sometimes when he should have been *at* school. The wrecked, burned out, rusted metal hulks stacked on top of one another fired his imagination. They were like a jumble of buildings on some other planet. He liked the feel of them, the cold sharpness of the steel, the soft texture of the seat stuffing spewing from rips and gashes. It all gave him a heart thumping feeling of excitement. He liked the curious shapes, caved-in panels, bits sticking out like the limbs of alien creatures. The heavy, metal smell, burned paint, gasolene, engine oil. He made the images stay in his mind so he could draw them later. He'd turn them into alien planets. War-torn cities, ruined buildings, people, blown to bits.

Sometimes he showed the drawings he had made to his art teacher at school.

'Umm.' Mr Mark would stare at them, then at him. Frowning. 'Umm,' he'd mutter again thoughtfully. 'Brilliant, Kee, but pretty gruesome.'

Kegan liked that . . . brilliant but gruesome. It was the nicest thing anyone had ever said to him. In fact that was how he thought of his life. Sometimes . . . like seeing the fox. Like messing around at the scrappies, brilliant. Sometimes . . . gruesome.

Part One

1

K egan's dad trawled his eyes away from the screen. It was Arsenal versus Manchester United. Clash of the Titans. Crowds chanting, roaring.

Kegan hated soccer. He hated the violence because it was real. Not like in the movies, or the sort he put on paper that didn't hurt anyone. He hated the swaying, chanting crowds. It all seemed so pointless, caring so much if a ball went between two posts or not. Odd for someone who'd been called after a footballer. He'd tried to like the game but he simply couldn't bring himself to care about it. He *had* liked it when he was a little kid. But then he began to see through all the brawling and arguing and swearing. Anyway, it reminded him too much of home.

'Where've you been?' his dad muttered when he realized Kegan was home and standing in the doorway.

Kegan leaned against the frame, shifting from one muddy trainer to the other. He shrugged. 'Nowhere.'

His dad lost interest. As far as he was concerned *anywhere* was nowhere if there weren't twenty-two blokes kicking a ball around on it.

'Where's Mum?'

'At work, where d'you think?' His dad didn't look up.

Mum worked in the processed food factory across the road.

'She on nights, then?'

''Course, stupid.' His dad took a swig of lager. 'She

ain't gone over there for a party, has she? Now get to bed, will you.'

Kegan opened his mouth to say he hadn't done his homework, or had any tea. But his dad wouldn't care. And anyway, Kegan hardly ever did homework. Most teachers had even given up asking.

In the kitchen, the sink was piled high with dishes. Kegan ran the hot tap, filled the bowl and washed them up. He dried them quickly, stacked them in the cupboard, then cleaned the sink. At least Mum wouldn't have that lot to come home to in the morning. He spread a few slices of bread with margarine and marmalade and took them upstairs.

On the way to his room he peeped in at Gary. Gary was two. He was called after a footballer too although Kegan wasn't sure which one.

He went to pull the blanket up over his brother's shoulders. He wrinkled his nose. The toddler's nappy needed changing. Trust Dad not to have bothered. He thought about trying to do it without waking the child then decided not to. He would probably cry, objecting to being disturbed. A sound that would bring Dad hurtling up the stairs like a herd of buffalo. Yelling as he always did, 'Can't you shut that kid up!'

The toddler's cheek was flushed. A bright spot the colour of cherries. When Kegan touched it, it burned under his fingertip. Kegan gave a sigh. Teething probably. At least it wasn't a bruise. He'd had a few from Dad already, poor little kid. Kegan's heart turned with pity. He'd have liked to scoop Gary up in his arms and run away with him. But he knew that was just a dream. Anyway, where could they go?

Gary's spiky hair was stuck to his forehead. He stirred under Kegan's light touch, his mouth making sucking motions. He'd loved his old bottle but Dad had chucked it away. 'Bloody thing!' he'd yelled when he tripped over it, picked it up and hurled it across the room.

Kegan felt guilty, leaving Gary alone with Dad. He hadn't remembered his mum was on night shift this week. She'd probably told him but he'd forgotten, or hadn't heard in the first place. He'd probably been off daydreaming somewhere in another universe. He'd been so anxious to see Slink again he hadn't given anything else a thought. Mum would go ballistic when she got home in the morning. Kegan would have been supposed to get the kid's tea, change his nappy, put him to bed.

In his room, Kegan sat by the window hunched against the cold. He ate his bread and marmalade. He thought about Slink. Where did she live? What did she eat? Why had she looked at him as if she could read what was going on in his head?

When he had finished he stowed the plate under the bed, stripped off and crept under the covers. Curled up you could be anywhere you wanted. Shafts of light from the street lamp carved a bright route across the peeling wallpaper. The patch of damp in one corner looked like a dinosaur devouring a bird. He thought about the fox again. He'd hardly thought about anything else all day. He'd gone to the yard again after school but there hadn't been any sign of her. Not even a soft paw print in the mud to tell him she'd passed.

There had been a van parked by the owner's caravan today. Two men were talking to the fat guy who ran the place. Borough Council Pest Control it said on the side of their vehicle. Kegan reckoned they'd come to get rid of the rats. There was a load of them haunting the yard in spite of the horde of feral cats that earned their living catching them. He'd seen the rats' grey, darting shadows. Heard high-pitched squeaks in the moonlight, bead-bright eyes catching the gleam. Kegan liked rats. They had a right to live, same as anything else. They were survivors. He'd read that if the human race was wiped out, rats would take over the planet. *Planet of the Rats.* He grinned to himself. Good title for a movie. They'd probably do better than mankind had done. He'd made the mistake of saying that to someone at school once and they'd laughed and called him Rat-boy, but he didn't care. Sticks and stones could break his bones but names could never hurt him.

'What you doing here, son?' the men from the van had said when they saw him saunter past.

Kegan had nodded in some vague direction. 'Waiting for my dad,' he'd fibbed.

'Well, be careful,' they warned. 'This is a dangerous place for kids to play.'

'Right.'

He'd watched them disappear round the corner, forgetting all about him.

The last thing Kegan saw in his mind's eye that night before he finally went to sleep was the fox again. She was resting now in a dark and secret place. She was curled up, her tail tucked right round to her ears like a built-in scarf to keep her warm. As if she knew he was thinking of her, she opened one eye and gazed at him then closed it again slowly before drifting off to sleep.

2

Mum had got in and gone straight to bed by the time he woke up the next morning. He scrambled out of bed anxious to be gone before his dad got up. He felt relieved Mum hadn't come yelling into his room to thump him for not being there for Gary the evening before.

On the way downstairs he peeped into his brother's room. The cot was empty, the blankets in a damp, acid heap at the end of the mattress. There was a dirty nappy on the floor. Mum must have changed him when she came in from work then taken him into her room. Cautiously he peered round their door. She was there, asleep, the child curled in the crook of her arm, his smelly cuddly blanket stuffed in his mouth. Dad was snoring like a mountain goat beside her.

In the kitchen Kegan helped himself to cornflakes, washed up and put away the bowl. The fridge was empty apart from a stack of beer cans so he grabbed a bag of crisps from the cupboard to scoff at lunchtime and left. Head down he walked against the snowy wind. His trainers let in the water and by the time he reached the school gates his feet were numb and squelching.

'No mac today, then, Kegan . . . ? You'll catch your death.'

It was Mr Mark on his mountain bike, skidding up beside him. He was wearing a cycling helmet and long black mackintosh cape over his rucksack. Kegan had seen him wearing it before. It billowed out behind him as he pedalled as if he was Dracula on two wheels.

Kegan shrugged inside his tatty anorak. 'Forgot,' he mumbled.

Mr Mark swung his leg over the saddle and walked the rest of the way with him. On both sides boys, girls ran, laughed, smoked, punched, screamed, pulled, and slid into school excited by the snow but anxious to be indoors to get warm.

'Your mum and dad coming to parents' evening?' the art teacher asked as he parked his bike and locked all three padlocks.

Kegan shrugged again. 'Dunno,' he fibbed.

He *did* know, of course. He hadn't even bothered to take the note home. He'd screwed it up and chucked it in the gutter, watching it bob and twist, white-water rafting down the drain.

They wouldn't have come anyway. Mum would be at work or at bingo and Dad hated schools. He'd hated his own and now he hated Kegan's. He wouldn't be seen dead near the place. Gran might have come if he'd mentioned it to her but he'd feel a right wally, his grandma coming when it should be your parents.

They were inside by now. Kegan was still staring at the floor; Mr Mark still staring at Kegan.

'Pity,' Mr Mark commented. 'I'd have liked to have talked to them about your work.'

'Yeah?' *Fat chance*, he thought inside his head.

'You know you're the best in your year.'

'Am I?'

'Streets ahead,' Mr Mark said. 'Most of the others think art's just a doddle, a chance to mess around.'

'Yeah,' Kegan said.

Visions of Mr Mark's art lessons crashed into his head. Brushes tossed around, paper made into darts . . .

jokes flying about. His class was full of nutters, all of them, well . . . most of them anyway.

Mr Mark was still frowning. 'Kegan . . . if . . . ?' he began. Then he stopped.

Kegan waited.

The teacher went to say something else then thought better of it. 'Nothing,' he said. 'Go and dry off before first period.'

Kegan felt a thump on his back. 'Hey! Rat-boy.'

The name had stuck.

It was Bodger, only his buddy because no one else wanted to be friends with either of them.

'What did *he* want?' Bodger asked as Mr Mark headed off towards the staffroom.

Kegan shrugged. 'Nothing much.' He didn't want to tell Bodger what old Markie Mark had said. He'd only scoff and take the mickey. A pack of giggling girls came charging down the corridor, pushing them both to one side.

Bodger sniffed and wiped his nose on the back of his hand. 'Twits!' he yelled at the top of his voice.

Kegan clenched his fists. He couldn't wait for the day to end.

By the time the bell went it was snowing hard. Kegan stepped out of school to a blizzard. He hitched his bag up higher on his shoulder, put his hood up and his head down. *Like Scott of the Antarctic,* he thought. Into the teeth of the blizzard never to be seen again.

'Goin' home?' Bodger trotted beside him trying to keep up with his long strides.

Kegan shrugged. 'Na.'

'McDonald's?'

Kegan shrugged again. 'No dosh.'

'I'll lend you some.' Bodger, short, red haired, known for being a cheat and always having money in his pocket, looked at him eagerly.

Kegan shook his head again as a tall girl with her hair tucked into the hood of a red duffle coat kicked through the snow, passing them. Through the gates a shiny four-wheel drive waited to pick her up. As she climbed in, the engine gunned and roared away in a shower of grimy slush.

Bodger nudged him. 'That's that new girl, Zoë, she's called.'

'Yeah?' Kegan stared after her.

'I saw her giving you the eye in the canteen.'

'Crap.' Kegan felt his cheeks flush. But he'd noticed too. He'd felt her gaze burning into the back of his skull. He'd flicked his hair out of his eyes, turned and stared back but she'd turned away. But he knew she'd been looking all the same. Anyway what would she want with a skinny thing like him? Girls liked good-looking boys with muscles and trendy gear, not rangy scruff-bags like him. The word was she'd been at a snobby school before coming to this one so she'd probably never seen anyone like him before.

'So? You coming or not?' Bodger nagged.

He shook his head. 'Sorry,' although he wasn't really.

He headed off down the road leaving Bodger ducking snowballs. He headed towards the outskirts of town. In the corner shop his fingers closed over a fifty pence piece. He'd lied to Bodger. He'd got enough to buy crisps and a Mars. He could have his tea at the scrappies.

The lane that led past the old gasworks and on towards the breaker's yard was narrow and grimy. Jagged bits of broken glass had been set into the top of the high brick wall that flanked the pavement.

The lane was a dead end. The scrappie's gate was open and a lorry, top heavy with crushed cars, was just pulling out. Kegan skirted sideways as it sliced through the wet snow then rumbled away, its load swaying dangerously. Right round the other side he had a secret way in between two loose panels of the high fence but he only used it if the gates were locked. It was dead easy to sneak past the owner's office caravan without being seen. Kegan was a dab hand at it.

Inside, he scuffed towards a pile of metal that had once been a yellow American saloon. He clambered inside and sat on what was left of the leopardskin covered passenger seat, gazing out. The snow was turning the sheltered parts of the yard into an alien world. It settled softly, nestling into the nooks and crannies of the wrecks, blunting the sharp steel edges and bleaching the rutted ground into a white carpet.

Hugging his knees for warmth, Kegan scoffed his crisps and Mars then dragged his art pad from his rucksack. He sketched the inside of the motor, eyes narrowed, making patterns from the twisted metal. He drew the dials and switches on the imitation walnut dashboard. The bent chrome steering wheel he turned into a space station.

Soon it was too dark to see. He stowed away his pencil and sat back with a sigh, hugging himself tighter, trying to get warm. It was great here—his own little world. His own little frozen world. Antarctica. The gates had closed long ago. He'd heard the hard grinding squeak of the reluctant hinges. The clanking of the great chain that linked them together squealed through the arctic air and echoed round the metal mountains. Kegan didn't have a watch but he knew it must be gone five. One thing Fatty, the owner, always did was close up on time.

In spite of the crisps and Mars, Kegan's stomach rumbled. He sat motionless, hardly daring to breathe in case the fox was near and the sound of his breath scared her away.

13

After a while it stopped snowing. The clouds disappeared and the moon came out. He was teeth-chatteringly chilled. He was bonkers to stay. He should get home before he died of the cold.

At last he tucked his pad back into his bag and clambered out. The snow was deep and crunchy under the soles of his trainers. White. Beautiful and eerie in the light from the risen moon. Then, suddenly, he knew he was no longer alone. There was a movement in front of him.

She had come.

Slink.

A flash of red against the white. A long soft pale-tipped tail, dark socks, pad marks in the snow. As she turned, moonlight caught the gleam of an eye, a pricked ear. Kegan held his breath. He could hear his own heartbeat. He could hear hers too. Faster than his. Two beats to one . . . in a rhythm. When he did let it out, his breath was like a grey ribbon of silk in the razor-sharp air. She was still staring at him, looking inside him just like she'd done before.

Then, suddenly, the vixen hunched her back, opened her mouth and gave a high, ghostly screaming bark. The sound bounced eerily round the yard and whirled into the sky sending its wild message across the rooftops and up to the stars.

Kegan shuddered. It was the most eerie, spooky sound he'd ever heard.

Then, from far away across the frozen streets and houses came an answer. A deeper fox bark. Echoing through the darkness like a message from another world. Slink sniffed the wind then as silently and as swiftly as she had come, she crept away and was gone.

Please come back. Kegan stood stock still, not daring to move. His eyes strained through the glistening moonshadows to catch another glimpse. He had wanted to try to touch her. To feel the soft warmth of her fur under his fingers. But it wasn't any good. She had gone.

3

When he got home the house was in darkness. He took the key from under the brick by the back door and went in. There was a note from his mum. Gary was round his gran's for the night. Dad could have gone to any one of the fourteen pubs in the locality.

He made himself beans on toast and sat in the front room, as close to the one-bar electric fire as he dared. He didn't switch on the light. The glare from the street lamp was enough. All he could hear was the distant hum of traffic, the scrunch of the toast inside his head. He liked it when there was no one else in the house. When it was quiet and dark. Sitting there in the shadowed room pretending he was elsewhere. Pretending he was with Slink, curled up somewhere, warm and safe.

Later, when he'd surfaced from his daydream, he washed his things up then went up to his room. There, he clicked on his lamp. The bare bulb spilled its hard light across the room. He dragged his pad out from his bag and began to draw her. It was easy. He could see her clearly as if his brain had taken a photograph. The pencil seemed to move across the page as if someone else was guiding it. The stippled fur of her back, her snowy white belly and chest, the black nose and scanning, amber eyes. Furry ears, pale inside and soft. Sharp whiskers, four dark socks, long, sweeping tail. The fox seemed to come to life as he drew her. Her coat rippled in the wind, her ears twitched, her eyes searched, ears turned for sounds, paws padded softly through the snowy landscape.

Eventually he sat back with a sigh of satisfaction. She was there on the page in front of him.

Slink.

Now he could keep her for ever.

When he heard his dad's key in the front door he pushed the pad down under the covers and clicked off the light quickly. The musty smell of the unheated room seemed to have soaked into the blankets. Kegan held a fistful close to his face. He heard heavy footsteps, heavy breathing, as his father hauled his enormous bulk up the stairs. His door opened.

'Kegan? You asleep, son?'

'Almost.' He tried to make his voice sound sleepy.

He screwed his eyes up tight as the light suddenly flared. His dad thudded in and sat down heavily on the end of the bed.

'What you been up to today?'

Kegan raised his head warily above the edge of the covers. Even from there he could smell the beery breath. He knew his father's good moods were always volatile. They could change into violent anger if he put a foot wrong. That was half the trouble really, when his dad smiled you got lulled into a false sense of security.

'Nothing much,' he said, then adding more hastily in case his dad exploded, unsatisfied with the answer to his question. 'Just maths and stuff as usual.'

His dad curled up his lip. 'Bloody maths,' he said. Then he dragged something from his pocket. It was an envelope. Kegan could see the typewritten name and address on the outside. Mr and Mrs B. Wilson . . . and the rubber stamp that said the name of his school. His heart turned in dread.

'Got this today.' His dad wrenched the letter from

the envelope and waved the white piece of paper at him like someone surrendering.

'Yeah?' Kegan tried desperately to sound calm. One of the teachers had written a letter once before and his dad had gone ballistic. The bruise had stayed on his backside for months, first a purpley blue, then green and brown. He'd just been able to see it if he screwed himself round and looked in the mirror. His father never hit him where the marks would show. He was far too crafty for that.

Kegan swallowed nervously. 'What's it say?'

'Some geezer called Adam Mark says he wants to see your mum and me.' His dad shifted and leaned towards him, so close Kegan could have got drunk on his breath. 'What you been up to?'

'Nothing.'

'Yeah? Pull the other one . . . '

'Honestly.' Kegan was so scared his heart seemed to be stuck in his throat.

'What's he want to see us for, then?' His dad leaned closer so that his face seemed magnified in the reflection of the boy's terror. 'You been bunking off again?'

'No, honestly.' Kegan felt he was shrinking, getting smaller and smaller, disappearing down under the bedclothes until there was nothing left of him but a frightened heartbeat. 'He's my art teacher.' His voice shook even though he tried not to let it. 'He already asked if you were coming to parents' night.'

'Art!' His dad sat back, screwed the letter into a ball and threw it at Kegan's face. It clipped his nose but he didn't flinch. 'Art—it's nothing but crap.' He leaned close again. 'Art won't get you nowhere,' he hissed.

Kegan heard the squeak of the bedsprings and felt the mattress rise as his dad got up. 'Tell the geezer we

18

ain't got time,' he said. 'Your mum works nights and I'm busy.'

'Yeah, OK.' Kegan breathed a silent sigh of reprieve as his dad went out and slammed the door. He waited until the heavy footsteps died away then felt around for the screwed-up paper. When he located it he tiptoed to the window and read it by the light of the street lamp. He hadn't dared put his light on again in case his dad heard and came storming back.

> Dear Mr and Mrs Wilson,
>
> I wonder if it would be possible for you to attend parents' evening on Thursday next as I'm particularly anxious to talk to you about your son, Kegan. As I'm sure you'll know, Kegan shows great artistic promise and I would like to talk to you about his future. I look forward to seeing you next week.
>
> Yours sincerely,
> Adam M. Mark.
> Head of Art.

Kegan's mind whirled. What was old Markie Mark on about? *Great artistic promise?* And didn't he know better than to write to his mum and dad? The geezer must be barmy.

But the words *great promise* just wouldn't go away. They whirled around in his head for what seemed like hours and hours. No teachers had ever said he showed *great promise* at anything before. All they had ever said was that he was lazy and tiresome and completely unable to concentrate for more than five minutes at a time and that they knew he could do better if he really tried. In other words, he was a waste of space.

When he heard his dad's footsteps on the stairs again he almost stopped breathing. He thought about those sci-fi monsters who could track down their prey merely by the sound of its heartbeat. He took deep breaths so his would calm down. When the footsteps stopped outside his door he squeezed his eyes and his fists up tight and held his breath until the footsteps went away. Then he tiptoed back to bed letting his breath out in a huge, silent sigh of relief.

Even after his dad's footfalls faded along the landing he still lay curled in a ball. It wasn't until he heard the thump and creak that told him his father had fallen into bed that he even began to relax. Even then sleep didn't come.

Once, he got up and gazed miserably out of the window. Shivering, he stared down at the empty street. It had snowed again. Everything was lumpy and white. Silent. The sky was inky blue, the stars a million sparking messages from space. He imagined he could see Slink, walking along the pavement then stopping to look up at him when he called her name. Wherever she was, he hoped she was warm. Curled up somewhere, her soft flowing tail wrapped round under her nose. He longed to see her again. To have her with him, to make her his own.

Crazy schemes invaded his head. Could he make friends with her? If he began taking her food she might learn to trust him. She might let him stroke her, run his fingers through her soft fur. She might even sit on his lap.

It must have been about three o'clock before he finally dozed off. And even then, images of Slink running through the snow to greet him haunted the edges of his mind.

4

'Kegan, this is excellent.'

He'd decided to take the picture of the fox to show the art teacher.

He went red. 'Is it?'

'Yes. You've really managed to make it come to life. Did you do it from a photograph?'

Mr Mark was touching the fur of her coat as if he could feel how soft it was.

'Er, no, I saw it . . . her.'

'Did you?' The man didn't look as if he believed him. 'Where?'

Kegan thought it better not to let on but he couldn't think of a lie fast enough. 'Just somewhere,' he said lamely.

Mr Mark could obviously see he didn't want to tell him. 'Well, it's brilliant. May I keep it?'

Kegan was torn. He'd like Mr Mark to have it but he'd vowed to keep it with him always.

'Er . . . ' he held his hand out for the drawing. 'I could do you another one.'

Mr Mark didn't give it to him. Instead, he said, 'Kegan, sit down a minute.'

Kegan sat, puzzled.

Mr Mark went to his briefcase and took out a file. 'Kegan, did you know an art scholarship exists at this school?'

Art scholarship? The teacher's words came out of the blue and Kegan didn't have a clue what the man was on about.

'What?' he muttered.

Mr Mark was used to his monosyllabic answers, silences, shrugs instead of words. 'A scholarship,' he repeated patiently. 'A woman who used to be a pupil here left money in her will to fund a scholarship to, every year, send one of our pupils to art college,' he went on.

'Yeah?'

'Did you see the letter I sent your parents?'

'Yeah.' He didn't say only because his dad had screwed it up in a ball and thrown it at him.

'I hoped it might persuade them to come to parents' evening.'

Kegan shook his head. 'They're too busy,' he lied.

Mr Mark sighed. 'Pity.' He opened the folder. 'I really wanted to talk to them about it. I'd like to put you in for it.'

'Me? You've got to be joking.'

'No, I'm not joking, Kegan. I'm deadly serious. If you were successful it would fund three years at college for you when you leave here.'

'College? Me? Don't be daft.'

Mr Mark was staring at him. 'Why not?'

Kegan shrugged. 'It's just daft, that's all.'

'Will you think about it?'

He knew it was hopeless, a dream, but was curious anyway. 'I dunno. What would I have to do?'

Mr Mark leaned forward. 'You'll have to present a portfolio of work to the Board who administer the fund.' He looked at the drawing. 'This would be a brilliant start. You could make wildlife your subject.' Kegan could see the art master's imagination was running away with him. 'Kegan, I'm certain you'll pass your GCSE next year and if you were awarded the scholarship you could do art in the sixth form, then go on to college.'

22

Kegan gazed at him. Suddenly he felt sorry for the man. He'd only been at the school a short while. He hadn't got a clue about Kegan. Not a clue.

Kegan got up. 'I wouldn't be allowed,' he said flatly.

Mr Mark sat back with a sigh. 'I could help you, Kegan. I *want* to help you.'

He shook his head. 'You don't understand. My dad thinks art's crap.'

Mr Mark looked exasperated. 'But surely he wants the best for you? Couldn't I just *talk* to him about it?'

Kegan stared at the master curiously. Was he deaf? Did the bloke come from another planet or something? 'No, you couldn't talk to him,' he muttered. 'It's him what does all the talking.' He put his hand out for the drawing. 'Sorry,' he said.

He knew Mr Mark was watching him as he went out. He knew he'd got a sorrowful, puzzled, look on his face. He was trying to help. Teachers had tried to help before. Social workers, too, once until Dad gave them the boot. But didn't any of them understand? No one could help. No one.

Later, Mr Mark found him in the school library searching for a book in the nature section.

'Kegan, I've had a word with the Head about you. Look, I'm sorry, I didn't mean to give you any hassle.'

'It's OK.'

Then he saw Kegan was holding a book about foxes. 'Have you got a thing about foxes?'

'Yeah, I suppose so. I think they're brilliant. I'm trying to find out what they eat.'

'I could have told you that.'

'Yeah?'

'Well, rabbits and mice, voles, earthworms . . . small rodents, birds . . . '

'Rats?'

'Yep. Rats as well, and urban foxes eat anything they can find in bins or on rubbish tips.'

'Oh.'

'Kegan, if you want to know more about the wild animals that live in town you could join the Urban Wildlife Group. Have you ever thought of that?'

Kegan gave him a withering look. He was just about to say that people like him didn't join things when he noticed someone else in the library, hovering between non-fiction and fiction and listening to their conversation. It was the new girl, Zoë.

'I couldn't help eavesdropping.' She came across. Her uniform was painfully new. Her long pale hair had been wound into a dozen or so plaits with a bead at the end of each one. She fiddled self-consciously with the end of one of them, twisting it round and round her index finger. 'When we lived in the country I had a pet fox,' she announced.

Kegan looked at her. 'Foxes ain't pets, they're wild.'

'Mummy found it after a hunt had killed its mother,' she explained. 'We brought it up.'

Mummy! Kegan thought. *That's a laugh.*

'That's very interesting,' Mr Mark said. He glanced at his watch. 'I'd love to hear all about it, Zoë, but I'm supposed to be somewhere else. Maybe you can tell Kegan . . . Kegan, I'll talk to you later about that scholarship.'

'Yeah, sure.' Kegan turned to Zoë. 'Who killed its mother?' Snobby or not, he was eager to get back to the subject of foxes.

'The hunt.' She stared at him with green eyes. He'd never seen anyone with eyes that colour before. 'The beastly hounds tore his mother to bits.'

Kegan shuddered. He had a sudden vision of Slink being chased until she dropped, then being torn to pieces.

'I don't know how anyone can kill *any* animal.'

She half-smiled. 'Neither do I. Mummy was furious. You should have heard the names she called them. We're terribly against blood sports. We think they're absolutely ghastly. The hunt rode roughshod over my grandfather's farmland without permission. He was livid.'

'I'd have shot 'em.' Kegan clenched his fists tight. 'All of 'em.'

Zoë laughed. 'A man after my own heart,' she said.

It seemed such a funny thing to say that he couldn't help grinning.

'I'll bring you some photographs of him if you like,' she said. He could see she was wary, still twisting the lock of hair. He wasn't surprised. Newcomers always got a bad time. Especially someone like her who looked and talked different to anyone else.

He said, 'I know where there's one.' The words were out before he could stop them. He realized he'd been dying to share the secret with someone. Mr Mark just hadn't been the right one.

'A fox. Really? Here, in town?'

'Yeah.'

'How wonderful.'

'Where's yours now?' he asked.

'We re-homed him with a man who runs a fox sanctuary,' she told him. 'He was too tame to ever go back to the wild. He didn't know how to hunt for food, you see.'

'Oh.' Kegan tried to imagine how she had felt when she had to give up her pet.

Zoë sighed. 'It broke my heart to little pieces when he went even though I knew he'd be much better off.'

'Yeah, I bet.' He really wanted to tell her more about Slink. He didn't really know why. He didn't have a clue whether he could trust her or not.

'Why do you want to know what they eat?' she asked.

'I'm going to feed mine,' he said. *Mine!* Slink had already become his.

'Why? Can't she get food for herself? Foxes are awfully good at finding food, even in winter.'

'I want to make friends with her.'

'It won't be easy. Foxes are very shy and wary of humans.'

He shrugged. 'I don't care, I'm going to try.'

'Some people hate them, you know.'

'What? Like those hunter people.'

'Oh, I don't necessarily think they hate them. They just love galloping about on horses and getting rid of foxes is a good excuse.' She tossed her hair back so her beaded plaits swung round, jangling together with dull, woodeny sounds.

'But they don't do no harm.'

'My sentiments exactly,' she said. He half smiled again at her strange way of talking. 'I wish you'd tell me where she lives,' she went on. 'I could help you try to make friends with her.'

He hesitated. Telling someone *about* Slink and telling them where she lived were two different things.

Then, making up his mind, he said, although he didn't know why, 'I could show her to you if you like.'

Her eyes lit up. 'Oh, yes *please*. It'll remind me of my darling Rudolph.'

He couldn't help grinning again. '*Who?*'

'Rudolph,' she said. 'We named him after Rudolph Nureyev. You know, the ballet dancer. Because he was so elegant.'

'Never 'eard of him,' Kegan chuckled.

5

'Right,' Zoë said. They were still in the library talking fox-talk when the bell went. 'When?'

'After school?'

'That would be lovely.' She rummaged in her bag then dragged out a mobile phone. She dialled. 'Mummy? Oh, hi. Look, I'll be late home today, I'm going somewhere with a friend. He knows where there's a wild fox and has promised to show me. No, it's all right. I won't be too late, honestly. Yes . . . I love you too.'

She grinned and powered down the phone. 'That's fixed.'

He stared at her. She really was weird. He'd have thought someone like her wouldn't be allowed to go traipsing off after school.

'Didn't she mind?'

'No, 'course not. She's delighted I've got to know someone. I think she'd given up. She's got this irrational horror of me not settling down in town and never making any friends. My old school was rather different to this one, you see.'

'Snobby, was it?'

She grinned. 'Frankly, my dear, yes, it was.' She waved and went off down the corridor.

Then, strangely, daydreaming during maths, he found he was looking forward to meeting her after school.

'My father died so we decided to move,' Zoë told him later

as they made their way down the muddy lane to the scrappies.

'Oh.'

'He had leukaemia, poor Daddy.'

'Oh.' He didn't know what else to say. *I wish it could have been mine and not yours,* wouldn't be right. She'd probably be shocked and never speak to him again. 'Why did you have to move?'

'Mummy wanted to get away. The memories at the cottage were too painful. She wanted to make a new start. She's a gynaecologist and was offered a good job at the hospital here.'

'A what?'

She gazed at him. 'A gynaecologist . . . a doctor . . . you know, deals with babies and wombs and stuff.'

'Oh,' he said.

'We knew it would be a culture shock but we're getting used to it.'

'Good.' He said that because he couldn't think of anything else.

'Why do they call you Rat-boy?' she asked suddenly.

'Because I was stupid enough to tell someone I liked rats.'

'Oh, I wondered, because you don't look a bit like one. I thought there must be some other reason. Why do you like them?'

'I like their eyes and their whiskers and because they're survivors.'

'I quite agree.' She laughed, her comment sounding as strange as when she'd said he was a man after her own heart. In fact, when he thought about it, a lot of things she said sounded weird. *Mummy* and *Daddy* and *I love you.* If she didn't watch out she'd be given a really hard time at school.

She strode on in front, not caring that the mud was

splashing over her expensive looking shoes and up the backs of her trousers. 'Come on, I'm totally dying to see your fox.'

She didn't even bat an eyelid when he took her through the scrapyard gates and told her to dodge down below the window level of the caravan. Past it, she straightened up and looked around, eyes wide with amazement. 'Goodness, look at all these wrecked cars. Mummy always says people drive like maniacs.'

He hadn't really thought of it that way.

She was still ahead of him. She had pushed back her hood and her plaits danced round her face. She stamped on a puddle of ice and smashed it to sharp triangles, stopping now and then to gaze up at the snow-capped metal mountains towering all around.

'There's so many!'

'Yeah.' He caught her up. 'Millions.'

'It's a wonderful place.' Her eyes shone again. 'Brilliant. Like being on another planet. We're Trekkies, are you?'

'Er . . . yeah.'

'*Star Trek*'s our all-time fave.' She rattled on without giving him a chance to answer or unravel his thought that dealing with wombs and liking sci-fi didn't really seem to go together. 'Do you come here a lot?'

'Yeah. Loads.'

'What for?' She walked beside him now, sloshing through the slush. Her shoes were covered but she didn't seem to notice.

Kegan felt shy. She'd think him a right idiot if he told her he loved the solitude. That the scrapyard was the only place where he could find peace of mind.

So he just shrugged. 'Just do,' he said.

He took her over to the Cadillac and they both

clambered in. Sitting on what was left of the upholstered seat, knees drawn up for warmth.

'This is wonderful,' she breathed. 'What an adventure.' She grabbed hold of the steering wheel and went brroom, brroom, the same noises Gary made when playing with his plastic car. Kegan thought she was nutty.

Already the January night was closing in around them. A cold mist was creeping from the frozen earth, swirling like phantoms through gaping windscreens and twisted, broken doors.

'What a totally fabulous place.' She gazed at him and he could just see the glitter of her eyes. 'I love snow, don't you?'

'Yeah.' He'd never met anyone before who felt the same as he did about it.

'It makes everything so beautifully virgin and clean.'

'Yeah. And cold.'

She laughed. 'And cold.' She undid her bag and rummaged about inside, pulling out files and books and pens and tissues and a small fluffy panda and a deceased computer pet. Eventually she came up with a packet of pink bubble gum. She handed him a bit.

'Ta.'

'Don't your parents mind you coming here?' she asked, chewing then blowing an enormous pink bubble that burst, covering her nose and mouth with transparent stickiness.

'They don't care what I do.' He watched her prise the gum from around her face and stuff it back into her mouth.

'Don't be silly, of course they do.'

She didn't know anything.

'No, they don't.'

She gazed at him curiously but didn't argue. She'd

probably never met anyone before whose *mummy* and *daddy* didn't care what they did. But she didn't comment. She just chewed, her jaws working furiously as if she'd got a mouthful of tough steak she couldn't get rid of. 'You should go in for that scholarship. That drawing you were showing Mr Mark was brilliant. I saw some others of yours pinned on the walls in the art room. They're excellent too. You should, you really should.'

He shrugged. How could he explain? Art didn't get you nowhere his dad had said. Well, *he'd* managed to get nowhere with or without it.

'Tell me about your fox,' he asked, changing the subject.

She was in mid sentence, telling him about how Rudolph had chewed Mummy's best slippers and they were both laughing when suddenly Kegan spotted a moonlit shadow emerging from the mist.

He put his hand on her shoulder. 'Shh! There she is.'

He heard Zoë draw in her breath. 'Wow,' she whispered. 'She's beautiful.'

'Her name's Slink,' he whispered.

'Slink.' The word seemed to settle softly on her lips. He heard her repeat it softly to herself. 'What a totally fabulous name.'

They watched for a while, hardly daring to breathe. Beside him, Kegan could feel the warmth of Zoë's shoulder. It seemed that her thick red duffle coat was keeping the cold away from them both. He glanced at her once. She was leaning forward, still chewing, a rapt look on her face.

The fox stood in front of them, tail swaying. She lifted her nose to the sky then barked her high, weird bark that Kegan had heard before.

31

'She's calling,' Zoë hissed in his ear.

'What for?'

'A mate, stupid.'

'Oh.'

Then another fox came padding silently in from nowhere. A bigger one this time. Broad chest, tawny face, black paws when he lifted them from the snow, tail raised, waving. Kegan swallowed. His heart was thudding so loudly he reckoned the drumbeats might scare them away.

The two animals sniffed one another warily. Then Slink crouched down, rubbing her face on the ground and round the bigger fox's front legs. She made strange little squealing noises in her throat. She plunged towards him, then darted back. He turned in circles, round and round, sending little blizzards of snow into the air. Slink jumped, all four feet off the ground at once, then darted away. He followed swiftly and they both melted into the shadows.

'What was all that about?' Kegan asked when he let out his breath.

'She was flirting with him. She thinks he's gorgeous but she's playing hard to get.'

'Oh.'

'If they mate then she'll have her cubs in the spring.'

He turned to her. 'Cubs? Brilliant.'

'If we can find out where her earth is then we'll be able to spy on them.'

'Her what?'

'Earth. It's what a fox's home is called.'

'Oh. Would it be here, in the yard?'

'Might be.' Suddenly Zoë shivered. She clambered out of the car and began walking around, stamping her feet. 'I'm freezing. Shall we go before we get hypothermia?'

Fatty was just closing up. He eyed them suspiciously. 'What you two kids doin' here?'

'We're looking for possible locations,' Zoë piped up.

Kegan didn't know what she was on about.

Neither did Fatty. 'What?' His nose was red with cold and his fleece jacket had greasy stains down the front.

'Locations for an art project,' Zoë fibbed.

'Well, can't you see that notice?' Fatty pointed to the sign over the gate. TRESPASSERS WILL BE PROSECUTED.

'Oh, we were going to ask permission but we couldn't find anyone.' Kegan was stunned how someone like her could lie so convincingly.

Fatty must have been impressed by her posh accent. 'Well, make sure you do next time,' he growled. 'This ain't a safe place for kids to wander around.'

'Thank you so much.' Zoë sailed through the gates with Kegan in tow.

Outside she burst into giggles and ran off in front. She turned. 'Come on, slowcoach. You can come home and have supper with me if you like.'

'Your mum won't want you bringing no one like me home,' he said when he caught her up.

'Don't be silly. What's wrong with you, anyway?'

He shrugged. 'Well, I'm a scruff-bag for one thing.'

'Don't be silly. She won't mind if you're not wearing any clothes at all.'

In the high street they shivered by the bus stop. The pavement snow had melted into puddles and the shop lights were another world in their reflection. Some of the windows still had their Christmas decorations up. They looked sad and incongruous now the season had gone.

Zoë stamped her feet. 'Hurry up, bus.'

'How much is it?' He only remembered he'd spent his fifty pence when they spotted the vehicle trundling towards them.

'Don't worry.' She fished in one of her pockets. 'I've got plenty.'

On the bus, he stared out at the passing shops and houses. The bus was heading out towards the posh end of town. Smart new estates, a sports centre. He'd been out there once with Bodger to muck around when it was all one big building site. Now he could see it was neat and tidy, big red-brick houses, smart gardens. Big cars in drives, two, sometimes three.

'I've got a good name for Slink's mate,' Zoë said when they were almost there.

'Yeah? What? Not Rudolph.'

She laughed. 'No, Red.'

'Rudolph the red-nosed reindeer?'

She laughed again. Louder. 'No, silly, just Red.'

'Red . . . ' He liked it. 'Yeah, OK.'

The bus stopped at the end of the road. She jumped off and waited for him. 'I could murder a cup of tea,' she said as they walked up the hill. She glanced at her watch. 'Mummy should be home by now.'

His heart sank as he stood at the gate. The house looked like one of those you see on the front of glossy magazines when you're buying the *Sun* for your dad. Detached. Mock oak beams. New. Clean. Warm. He just didn't belong in a place like this.

'Come on, Kee, for goodness' sake.' Zoë was already unlocking the front door.

His courage deserted him. 'No.' He shook his head. 'It's OK, I'd better get home.'

She toddled back up the path and grabbed his hand. 'Don't be a moron. Come on.'

6

Inside was a surprise. Half their stuff was still packed in boxes. The other half strewn everywhere. There were bare floors of polished wood and a huge picture of a woman with no clothes on sitting by a forest pool, propped up against the wall. 'We'll get round to unpacking everything one day.' Zoë had dismissed it all with a wave of her hand as they stepped round things to go through to the kitchen. He caught a glimpse of a huge front room with a carpet and an overstuffed settee sitting next to a piano, a tall potted plant and more boxes mostly of books. He couldn't see a TV anywhere.

He wanted to shrink into the ground when she said, 'His nickname's Rat-boy,' as she introduced him to her mother.

Anna, she had insisted he called her that and not Mrs Er . . . , frowned. 'That's not very complimentary.'

'I don't mind,' Kegan muttered into his chest. 'I like rats.'

'He says they're survivors and he likes all wild animals anyway.' Zoë was making tea. 'If you'd said you liked tigers you might have got called Tiger-boy,' she chuckled.

'You're right about rats. They are survivors.' Anna was staring at him. He didn't look her in the eye but he could feel she was. He imagined she was wondering how on earth her daughter had picked up such a scruff-bag.

'We're starving.' Zoë plonked a mug of hot tea in front of him. 'What's for tea?'

Just then, from somewhere amidst the boxes, the phone rang.

'Anything you fancy.' Anna took her mug and went to answer it.

Zoë opened the door of the biggest fridge he'd ever seen. It was crammed full of more food than the shelves in Sainsbury's. 'Cheese on toast with scrambled egg?'

His mouth watered. 'If you like.'

She shouted. 'Mummy, cheese on toast?'

'Yes, please,' the answer came back.

While they were eating, Anna asked, 'Did you manage to see the fox?'

Between mouthfuls, Zoë told her all about Slink and Red and the plan to try to find their earth.

'And Kee wants to put food out so she begins to trust us. May we have that left-over chicken?'

'Of course you may, darling.' *Darling!* Kegan squirmed. 'You might be successful, urban foxes are much more used to humans than the countryside variety.'

'Thanks, Mummy.' Zoë got up and gave her a hug. Kegan watched curiously, the two pale-haired heads so close together. 'We'll take it after school tomorrow, Kee, shall we?'

'If you like,' he mumbled.

'What do your parents think of your scheme?' Anna disentangled herself and got up to clear the dishes.

'Oh, don't ask,' Zoë said before he could mumble an answer. 'They don't care what he does. He doesn't even think they'll let him go for the art scholarship and he's so brilliant at drawing. You should see the one he's done of the fox. Have you got it in your bag? Go on, show Mummy.'

'What art scholarship?' Anna asked.

'One at school. Go *on*, Kee, for goodness' sake.'

36

Kegan wished a big hole would appear and swallow him up. He squirmed again at the curious, kindly way Anna was gazing at him. Reluctantly he took out the drawing and handed it to her.

She drew in her breath. 'It's beautiful, Kegan. What scholarship is my garrulous daughter talking about?'

'It's—' Zoë began but her mum interrupted. 'Let Kegan tell me himself, darling.'

He shrugged. 'It ain't nothing really.'

'Kee! It's not nothing at all.'

'Zoë!' her mum warned.

She poked him. 'Go on, tell her then.'

While he was telling her, Zoë got up and began to load the dirty plates into an already full dishwasher, stuffing them in as best she could then slamming the door and switching it on. It hummed and whirred, plates and glasses clanking together like a rock band.

Anna drew up a stool next to him, so close he could see the darker roots of her blonde hair and tiny reflections of himself in her eyes. He shifted back a little, afraid she'd smell he hadn't had a bath for ages. 'Kegan, it's wonderful to have a gift like this . . . you must make the most of it.'

He managed to hold her stare. He was puzzled that she cared so much. She'd only known him five minutes.

He sniffed and wiped his nose on the back of his hand. 'I couldn't go to college.'

'Why not?'

He lowered his gaze. 'Dunno.'

'Exactly.' Zoë was triumphant. 'You don't know because there isn't a reason.'

He got off his stool. 'I've got to go.' Suddenly the walls seemed to be closing in on him. What was he doing in this alien place where no one could even begin to understand?

It took an hour to walk home. By the time he got there he was frozen.

Mum was in the front room watching TV. Gary, back from Gran's, was asleep in Dad's chair.

'Where's Dad?' Kegan asked, appearing in the doorway.

'Away match,' his mum said. 'Gone with his mates. He'll be back tomorrow.' She turned to stare at him. 'Where you been?'

'Tea with a friend.'

His mum snorted. 'Yeah? Who? Not that ginger kid?'

He shrugged, not wanting her to know. 'No, just someone at school.'

She patted the seat beside her. 'Kee, I haven't seen you for days. Come and tell me what you've been up to.'

He felt a flush of pleasure. Maybe for just one evening it could be like before Dad came back. The time when there had just been the two of them and the occasional boyfriend of Mum's. When he was little and a good kid and not scared all the time.

'Nothing much.' He fibbed. Even if he told her . . . asked her about the scholarship, she probably wouldn't listen.

'As usual.' She lit another cigarette.

'It's nice without Dad.' He settled himself beside her.

His mother sighed. 'Don't be like that, Kee. I know he's rotten to you sometimes but he can't help it. You know he gets depressed.'

'Yeah? Well, *I'm* depressed when he's around.'

'Kee, he *is* your dad.'

'Then why wasn't he here when I was little?'

She sighed again, exhaling cigarette breath. Her clothes smelt of the food factory where she worked—a mixture of curry and onions and cooked minced meat. 'You know why, Kee.'

'Prison, yeah, but why didn't he stay out of bother if he had you and me.' He was clenching his jaws together, the familiar anger welling up inside him before he could swallow it back down.

She sighed again, louder this time as if she was letting all the troubles of the world escape. 'God knows. Habit, I suppose.'

Kegan swallowed and drew his courage around him like a cloak. She was in a good mood. Why not ask her?

'Mum?'

'Ssh.' Bad timing, her favourite soap was just starting.

'Mum, I wanted to ask you something.'

She frowned and drew away from him. 'What now, Kee? You're always on about something.' It wasn't true. He hardly ever spoke to her unless she asked him a question. 'Oh, blimey, look at her hair!' she exclaimed at the blonde barmaid in the low-cut leopardskin top.

He bit his lip. 'Mum?'

She turned, exploding. 'Kegan, for God's sake shut-up. Go to bed if you're not going to let me watch in peace.'

Gary stirred again and sat up. He wiped the sleep from his eyes. His face crumpled and he began to cry.

'Oh, God, don't you start too!' Kegan's mum bent and lifted the toddler up. She handed him to Kegan. 'Stick him in his cot, will you.'

Wearily he got up. He felt as if he was retreating inside himself. He had to think about something good or else he'd scream. He took Gary into the kitchen and filled his feeding mug with warm milk and rammed on the lid. The toddler snatched it, stuffing it into his mouth greedily. Through tears, he smiled at Kegan between sucks. Kegan wiped the moisture from his brother's cheeks with his thumb then picked him up and took him upstairs.

The rooms were like ice. He put Gary into his cot and tucked the covers round him.

'Don't kick 'em off or you'll get hypothermia.' He dropped a kiss on the toddler's forehead. He stood watching for a minute or two as the child sucked at the almost empty cup, his fair lashes softly brushing his flushed cheeks as he fell into a doze.

In his own room, Kegan didn't even bother to undress. He felt angry and stupid. Why had he tried to tell her about the scholarship when all along he knew it wouldn't have been any good? He must be going off his head.

He crept under the covers and whispered to himself, 'See Markie, see Zoë, see Anna. Told you.'

7

'She's really put on weight.' Zoë took a bite of her chocolate bar. They were waiting for the foxes to appear. It was early. A Saturday morning with a ruby sky full of the promise of spring.

Waking at dawn, walking eagerly down the street with his pockets stuffed with stale bread, Kegan thought the sky looked as if it was on fire. He imagined a holocaust up there, cities burning. The clouds streaked with terror.

'You reckon?' Kegan sat hunched beside her.

'Definitely. Gestation is around fifty-three days. I looked it up.'

He turned to her. '*What's* fifty-three days?'

'Gestation, Dumbo, Rat-boy. *Pregnancy.*' She screwed up her chocolate wrapper and tried to stuff it down the neck of his anorak.

'Hey, watch it, Zo!' He tore the paper away from her and they wrestled, giggling and shrieking.

Suddenly sober. 'Hey, shut-up, you'll scare her.'

'Me!' But she went quiet anyway.

Outside the fox earth they'd put a pile of food they'd brought with them. Kegan's bread, stale cake, some minced meat Zoë had brought. A few apples. They sat some way off, waiting.

Kegan had found the earth one evening quite by chance. Zoë had got a violin lesson so he went to the scrappies by himself. Fatty had been talking to someone by the main gates so he'd crept in through the loose

41

fence panel that divided the yard from the narrow street that ran along to the old railway goods depot. He had been sauntering along when he suddenly spotted her. Slink. Emerging from a hole in a pile of soil and rubbish banked up against the fence in a part of the yard that was hardly used any more. He'd halted, his breath dying in his throat. The vixen had looked around warily, only seeing him as she turned to steal away.

'Hi.'

He had whispered to her as she stared at him. Looked through him. Inside him. She heard his heartbeat and knew he was her friend. He had crouched down, holding out the stale bread he'd brought but she wouldn't come near. 'Please.' He longed to feel the softness of her muzzle against his fingers. His heart had pounded as she swayed to and fro, uncertain whether to stay or flee. She raised her nose. He knew she could smell the food. Her eyes had been amber-bright in the dim evening light.

As he watched, Slink had sat down and begun to wash herself. Slowly, as if she was giving him a demonstration of how to do it. He wondered if perhaps she wasn't hungry. If she had feasted earlier on someone's chickens or beetles dug up from the ground round the elder tree that grew through the fence on the other side of the yard, or rats chased and caught when they least suspected it. Then he spotted Red some way off. He was coming swiftly down one of the alleyways between the wrecks. Something hung from his jaws. A soft bundle of brown feathers, a lolling head with a blood-bright cockscomb dangling.

Kegan had stepped back into the shadows as Red went by. He saw the big dog fox lay his offering in front of Slink. She left off washing herself and stood up making little whining sounds in her throat. Then she lay down on her stomach with her legs splayed out behind and began chewing the head off the chicken. When she had finished most of the carcass she began washing herself again while Red gobbled up what was left. Then they went off together, heads close, tails high and waving like feathers in the wind, as if they were discussing the day's news.

Zoë had been over the moon when he told her about the earth.

'That means she's definitely pregnant. She only chooses her home a week or so before the cubs are due.' She had jumped up and down. 'Oh, I wish I'd been there. I knew she was putting on weight.' To his horror she'd flung her arms round him and hugged him. 'And Red is so good to her. Such a brilliant husband. Isn't it stupendous?'

'Yeah.' He never could help grinning at the funny things she said. 'Stupendous.'

Since then they had come every day although it had been a week since they had seen Slink. Red had been going in and out with food, but there hadn't been a sign of the vixen.

Kegan was getting fed up with waiting. 'I wish they'd 'urry up and get born.'

'I think they are getting born.'

He turned. 'Honestly?'

'Yep. She's in there with them now, I bet.'

He frowned. 'When are we going to see them, then?'

'Oh, they won't come out for ages, we'll have to be patient.'

They'd waited but there was no more coming and going.

Zoë got up. 'Come on, let's listen.'

They crept towards the earth, getting down on hands and knees. Ears close to the ground. Kegan could smell the metallic dry smell of the soil and feel the hard stones beneath his cheek. He held his breath, straining to catch the tiniest of sounds.

'Nothing.' Zoë sat up.

But Kegan could hear something. Little snuffles and squeaks, the sound of Slink's gentle growl—more like a cat's purr than anything else.

Zoë nudged him impatiently. 'What?'

He made her put her ear to the same place. He waited as he saw her face change from impatience to joy.

'Wow!' When she looked up her eyes were bright with tears. 'I can hear them,' she whispered. 'I can hear the cubs.'

Then, a few metres away they saw Red. He was staring at them. The long, naked tail of a rat hung from his jaws.

'Breakfast,' Kegan whispered. He caught Zoë's hand and pulled her up. 'Come on, let's go.'

They crept away, looking back once just in time to see the pale tip of Red's tail disappearing down into the ground.

There was a council van by the gates. Two blokes were deep in conversation with Fatty.

None of them spotted Kegan and Zoë skirting round a lorry full of scrap that had just arrived. Slipping out they laughed and ran up the lane, whooping and hollering.

At the top they were both red in the face.

'Cubs!' Zoë's grin was from ear to ear. 'I can't wait to tell Mummy.'

Going home he felt great. He wondered how many there were. Three. Four. Five. They'd have to think what to call them. Amber. Star. Kirk. Names barrelled through his head.

The first time he saw them was during the holidays.

44

Zoë had gone to stay with her grandfather on his farm. She had invited Kegan to go too but he knew it hadn't even been worth asking. Anyway, he'd stick out like a sore thumb in the country with her posh grandad. It had taken him long enough to pluck up courage to look her mum in the eye, let alone some old geezer who'd no doubt think he was a waste of space just like his dad did.

Zoë hadn't really wanted to go either.

'Yeah, but you might see some foxes there,' Kegan had said, trying to cheer her up.

She'd given him one of her withering looks. 'Yes, stupid, but they won't be *ours*, will they?'

That morning he'd got up at the crack of dawn. Something had made him wake up but he wasn't sure what it was. He'd got a tune on his brain, music he'd heard from downstairs the night before when his dad had been watching a horror movie with the volume turned up full blast. He'd gone out before anyone else was up.

It was quiet where the foxes had their earth. A place where most of the scrap had been cleared and no one came there any more. Sometimes Kegan had spent the whole day there, just sitting with his sketch pad, drawing, waiting, hoping that today might be the day the cubs came out for the very first time.

By now, he'd got a whole collection of drawings he'd done at the yard. Sometimes he'd sit in his room and go through them one by one. Zoë had said they'd be good enough for the scholarship. Getting it was now top of his daydream list. Even above seeing the cubs or punching his dad when he was having a go at Mum or getting some decent stuff to wear. He'd lie in bed imagining himself at college, living in a flat somewhere on his own a million miles away where there was no one to take the mickey or tell him what to do or yell and shout and throw stuff around.

Before Zoë went to her grandfather's she had said, 'Don't you ever think about what you want to do when you leave school?'

He'd shrugged.

'I do. I'm going to be a vet. I think about it all the time. I don't see the point in living if you haven't got a dream. And if you have got one, Kee, you've got to do everything to try to make it come true.'

He'd thought a lot about what she'd said. Maybe he *did* give up too easily. Trying to talk to his mum. Trying to be brave enough to stick up for himself.

He was thinking about it again when Slink's cubs ventured into the light for the first time. Their appearance took him by surprise.

First, Slink. Blinking in the early spring sunshine as if she had never seen it before. She looked thin and out of condition. Her coat was dull and matted, looking after a family had taken its toll.

Then a small black nose appeared. Next a rounded muzzle, a pair of wary eyes. Finally the first, dark red cub hauled itself into the world.

Kegan drew in his breath sharply, then, scared to let it out in case they heard and disappeared again, he sat as if frozen in time.

After that another. Then, eventually, a third. The last one was smaller, tiny, and more wary, peering, blinking, eyes scanning for danger as if scared to face the world. Kegan knew exactly how it felt.

He sat still as granite, scared that if he moved, or even breathed, he would frighten them back underground. It seemed the whole world was standing still, every part of it afraid to turn or move or breathe in case the cubs got scared and disappeared.

The cubs sniffed the air. They stuck close to Slink, wary of the huge landscape they'd ventured into. They looked around, then up at the sky as if they wondered what this bright blue ceiling was above their heads. One cocked its head as a flock of pigeons flew overhead, staring at them in amazement.

The biggest grew braver and wandered a little way away. It sniffed the ground, pawing at a stone, touching it with his nose. The second one chased after it and soon they were biting and barking in mock battle, tumbling and squealing in the dirt. The little one cowered close to its mother. It held one of its front legs in a strange way and Kegan saw it was deformed, hanging limply as if it was injured in some way.

Slink sat still, watching the two cubs play. She knew Kegan was there. She knew he had waited for this moment and was showing him it had been worth while.

He put down his pad and pencil softly and drew a bag of crusts from his pocket. He wished he'd brought some meat, she always came quickly for that. She'd run towards him, never for one minute taking her eyes from his face. Snatch the meat from where he or Zoë had placed it then run back, turning once as if to say 'thanks' then disappearing underground.

Today, though, as Kegan held out his fistful of bread she carried on staring at him. Then she slowly rose and moved towards him. The tiny cub limped after her, scared to be left on her own. The others, seeing their mother move, scampered behind her, stopping dead and looking at him with their bright eyes. Maybe she had told them about the two humans who came to feed them but would never harm them. Others would if they got the chance, but these two . . . never. The whole universe seemed to stop and the air shiver and shimmer around

47

him as he suddenly realized she was only a metre away from his outstretched hand. He had never imagined she would dare to come so close. He held the bread palm upward towards her and tried to stop his hand from shaking with excitement. She was so close now he could see each whisker, the light in each amber eye, the dark shadows inside each cocked ear. The cubs stood stock still as if they were frozen in time too.

It seemed to Kegan that the whole world was holding its breath.

Then, suddenly, the vixen darted forward, snatched the food and ran back. She dropped the crust beside the cubs. They dived at it in a dark red, furry mass of ears and paws and tails. Even the little one tried to join in.

Kegan took the rest of the bread from the bag. Would she come again? But it seemed she'd been brave enough for one day and he had to content himself with chucking it on the ground then retreating to sit again and watch. His heart slowed its wild beat. Wait until he told Zoë this!

By the time he left, he'd captured the cubs on paper. Star, the biggest and boldest, was jumping into the air after a bumble bee, all four dark paws off the ground. Kirk, the second, was rolling over in the dirt, and Amber, the littlest, was sitting close to Slink while she watched the others, her strange deformed leg held off the ground. Red was there too, striding down one of the alleyways, jaws full of something smelly he'd gleaned from someone's rubbish bag. The big dog fox had appeared suddenly, ignoring Kegan although he knew he was there. He flicked his eyes at him as he passed, accustomed now to seeing the human he too had learned to trust.

Dawdling home Kegan's heart was full of excitement.

He couldn't wait for Zoë to get back. She'd be sorry she'd missed the cubs' first entry into the world.

He stopped off at his gran's on the way home. He hoped it wasn't one of her bingo afternoons. If she was in he'd get a Coke and maybe a bit of home-made cake if he was lucky. Gran had got a soft spot for him. She'd looked after him all the time when he was little and his mum was at work and always found time to listen to what he'd got to say.

When he turned up she was in the kitchen of her terraced house in the street that went right under the railway arches and out the other side.

'Well, you're a stranger,' she remarked when he appeared. She was sitting in the kitchen smoking a fag and checking her football pools. 'Thought you'd forgotten your old gran.'

''Course not.' He put his sketch pad on the table and went to look in the larder. 'Got any cake?'

She gazed at him. 'You look as if you could do with a good meal not a bit of cake.' She was always on about him being skinny. She grumbled on about young people eating junk but got the tin out and cut him a slice of fruit cake anyway. Gran always grumbled on about everything but didn't mean half of it.

'Thanks, Gran.'

'Been drawing?' She picked up his sketch book before he could grab it. She opened it, flicking up the pages, staring at each one. He watched her face as she slowly scrutinized each picture. First Slink, then Red, then the snowy scrapyard with both foxes hunting. Then Zoë with her plaited hair sitting with her knees drawn up while Slink scoffed a chicken carcass she'd brought for her. Then Star, Kirk, Amber, limping along behind. Others were of a flock of seagulls that swarmed over the dump behind his house, a hop of sparrows gleaning crumbs in

49

the play park, one of a cat sunning herself on the wall of his back yard.

His gran sucked at her false teeth, going back and looking all over again. 'School work, is it?'

He shrugged. 'Not really.'

'Your mum seen these?' She didn't look up.

'No.'

She looked at him now. 'Why not?'

He shrugged. 'Dunno. She's too busy I s'pose.'

'What, looking after that pig she's married to?' Gran and his dad had always hated one another.

Kegan shrugged again. 'Yeah . . . and Gary.'

'How is the little darlin'? Seemed as if he was coming down with a cold when I saw him the other day.'

'He's fine.'

'Good. What about your teacher?' Gran pointed at his sketch pad. 'He seen these drawings of yours?'

He shook his head. 'Nah . . . well . . . some of 'em.'

'Well, *someone* should see 'em all.' She closed the book. 'You were always good at drawing, ever since you could first hold a crayon.' She sighed. 'God knows where you get it from.'

'I don't get it from anywhere. It's just me.' He'd got that from Zoë. She said everyone had something special they could do, you didn't have to get it *from* anyone. It was just you.

'Where do you see 'em?'

'What? The foxes?' There didn't seem any harm in telling Gran. She wasn't likely to go there, scaring them away.

'At old Charlie's scrapyard!' She stubbed her fag out and lit another one. 'That's funny, I read something about that place last week.'

'What, the scrappies?'

'Yeah. Something about part of it being sold off.' She rummaged through a pile of papers and magazines on a stool by the fireplace. 'Here.' She thrust a copy of the local paper at him.

The headline seemed to jump off the page.

It was the second time that day that the world seemed to shiver and shake. 'Half Breaker's Yard to Go in Bid to Build New Factory Units.' The print blurred in front of his eyes as he read the rest of the story.

'What's it say?' Gran was staring at him. 'I've forgotten now.'

'The half of the yard that backs on to the old railway works has been sold,' Kegan told her bleakly. 'They're going to build new factory units.'

'Factories!' Gran lit another fag. 'Ain't we got enough industry round 'ere? It's parks for you kids to play in we need, not bloody factories.'

Kegan hardly heard what she was saying. All he could hear was a drumming in his ears. Slink and Red and the cubs . . . their earth was in the part of the yard that had been sold. He scanned the story again, quickly, his eyes darting along the lines of words. Planning permission had been granted and work would start soon. He felt icy with fear. If they moved in with the JCBs and started building, Slink and her cubs would be killed for sure.

There was only one thought in his head. He *had* to tell Zoë.

'Zo?'

'Kee? Is that you?'

'Yeah. Listen, something's happened.'

It had taken ages to track down Zoë's mum so he could get her grandfather's number. He'd begged money

51

from Gran, run to the phone box down the road and quickly dialled her number. There wasn't any answer. He stood in the phone box, wondering what to do. He couldn't phone her mobile because he didn't know the number. He couldn't try to phone Anna at the hospital because he didn't know that number either. There was nothing else for it but to go there and ask to see her. They'd paged her from the reception desk and she'd come hurrying down the shiny corridor in her white coat, a half worried smile on her face.

'I need Zoë's phone number at her grandad's.' He was out of breath from running. 'It's really important.'

Anna had made him calm down. 'She's just phoned to say they're back. You could only just have missed her.'

Swearing, he'd dashed to the pay phone in the hospital's reception area and rung her at home.

'What?' Zoë must have known it was something urgent otherwise she would have rattled on about what she'd been doing before he could get a word in edgeways.

She gasped when he told her about the cubs.

'That's wonderful, I can't wait to see them.'

Then he told her the rest.

'They can't do that!'

'Well, they're going to.'

'Then we've got to save Slink and her cubs.'

'I know, but how?'

'I don't know, but there's got to be a way!'

8

'You're never here when I want you!' His mum was sitting at the kitchen table when he got home. Her friend Dawn was there, smoking too, the butts in the ashtray in front of her streaked with her scarlet lipstick. Gary was fretful, lying on the lino floor with his head on his cuddly, one corner of it stuffed in his mouth. His cheeks were flushed.

'What did you want?' Kegan didn't look at Dawn. He hated the way she eyed him up and down as if he'd just crawled out from a drain. He shuffled his feet in the doorway, anxious to get to his room, think, make plans about saving the foxes. Schemes were already tumbling through his head. Could they capture them and take them somewhere safe?

Mum stubbed out her cigarette and bent to pick Gary up. 'The baby's got a temperature,' she said, smoothing the child's flushed brow. 'He needs some Calpol.' She nodded her head towards her purse lying on the worktop. 'Pop down the chemist and get some, will you.'

Kegan came in and touched his brother's cheek. The kid was burning up. 'What's up with him?'

'Just his teeth. You going or not?'

'Ain't Dad here? He could have gone.'

'Cheeky little so and so,' Dawn muttered, lighting one fag from the end of the one she'd just finished. 'Why don't you kids do anything without arguing?'

Kegan ignored her.

His mum tutted. 'He's in bed, sleeping it off. Where d'you think?'

Kegan wasn't surprised. A taxi driver had dumped his father on the doorstep last night, then banged on the door for his fare. He'd heard the rumpus and stuck his head under the pillow.

Kegan took two pound coins from the purse and ran all the way. He felt a wave of anger. Why couldn't *she* have gone? Was sitting smoking with your mates more important than your kid's health?

Hurrying back, a gang from school was kicking a ball round in the road.

'Hey, Rat-boy. Been shopping for Mummy?'

He put his head down, not looking, not answering. He heard them laugh and jeer. At school they'd noticed his friendship with Zoë and never let it rest. But he didn't care. For the first time in his life he felt like a winner.

Almost home, a vehicle drew up behind him.

'Kee! I made Gramps drive me over.' It was Zoë.

Sitting in the driver's seat of the sleek, green Jaguar was a man, greying at the temples and suntanned. He raised his hand. 'Hi, Kegan.'

Kegan swallowed and said 'hello' but nothing came out but a squeak.

Zoë leaned back and opened the passenger door. 'Get in. We have to make plans.'

'Can't. My brother's sick, I've got to get this home.' He held up the carrier containing the bottle of medicine.

Zoë frowned. 'Can you possibly come later?'

He shrugged and mumbled. ''Spect so.'

'What's wrong with your brother?'

'Teeth, Mum said.'

'Poor darling. Please come as soon as you can.'

He watched the Jaguar speed away.

When he got back, Dawn had gone. Mum was still nursing Gary at the kitchen table. The toddler lay at a crooked angle in her arms, his head held stiffly as if he'd strained a muscle in his neck. He'd vomited and a soiled towel lay on the floor by her feet.

She looked up as he came in.

'I think he's got flu.' He could tell his mum was worried. Her voice was all wobbly and weak.

'Flu? That's serious for little kids, ain't it?'

'Yes.' Mum looked at him and he saw a sharp pinprick of fear in her eyes. 'What we going to do?'

He opened the bottle of medicine and poured some on to a teaspoon. He tried to put it into Gary's mouth but the toddler gagged and vomited again.

Kegan wiped his brother's mouth with the end of his cuddly. 'I'll go next door and phone the doctor.'

Mum pulled a face. 'You know old Mrs Gravina hates us.'

He didn't give a toss about Mrs Gravina hating them. If she didn't let him use the phone he'd just barge in and use it anyway. 'I'll tell her the baby's sick. Where's the number?'

'I don't know . . . somewhere in the drawer.'

He ransacked through, turning out bits of paper, old, unpaid bills, string, boxes of matches, bottle openers, until he found a list of doctor's surgery hours and telephone numbers.

He ran out, down the path and through next door's gate. He hammered on the front door then heard old Mrs Gravina shuffling up the hallway. 'Who is it?' she called.

'It's Kegan from next door. Please can I use your phone, the baby's sick.'

'Go use someone else's.' She'd always been stroppy since Dad dismantled a car's engine by the kerb in front of her house, then left it there to rot.

'There isn't anyone else.' He felt like kicking the door down. 'Please, Mrs Gravina, I'll pay for the call.'

There came the rattling of chains and bolts being undone. The door opened a crack. 'What's wrong with the baby?'

'Flu. He's really sick.'

The smell of frying, mothballs, and cat wee hit him as she opened the door wide enough to let him in. 'All right, but don't you touch anything.'

'I won't, honest.' He didn't know why the old bag thought he might want to.

The phone was in the front room on a table beside a settee so stuffed with cushions and piled with so many old, yellowing newspapers it looked as if she had been collecting them for years. The curtains were drawn together and the fire was blasting heat. Three cats stared at him with green eyes as he went in. He'd suffocate if he stayed there too long.

Mrs Gravina hovered by the door as he dialled the number.

'You'll have to bring him to the surgery,' the receptionist said.

'I can't, he's really sick and we'd have to come on the bus.'

'Oh, OK.'

Next thing he heard a man's voice asking him to describe Gary's symptoms.

A minute's silence, then, 'Can you get him to hospital?'

Hospital? He felt a knife of fear slice his stomach. 'Er . . . no.'

'Right.' There was a horrible urgency in the doctor's tone. 'Tell me your address and I'll send an ambulance.'

He knew his voice was shaking as he told the doctor where to send it.

Mrs Gravina hovered by the door as he rushed past. 'What he say?'

'He's got to go to hospital.'

Her hand flew to her mouth. 'Oh, *mama mia*.'

He didn't hang around to hear any more.

When he got back, Mum had put Gary in his cot. She went pale when he told her about the ambulance and for a minute he thought she'd pass out. 'I'll get him,' Kegan said.

Mum's hands were shaking as she lit a cigarette and exhaled sharply, filling the air with smoke. 'I'll wake your dad.'

'No.'

'What do you mean, no?'

There wasn't time to argue. 'Leave him, he can't do nothing. I'll come with you.' He didn't think he could stand it if his dad came and made trouble at the hospital.

But the ambulance siren woke him anyway.

'Wass goin' on?' he slurred as he thumped down the stairs. The paramedics were just taking Gary out, wrapped in his grimy blanket. Dad stood there scratching first his stomach, then his head.

There wasn't time to explain but he insisted.

'The baby's sick,' Kegan shouted. 'What do you think's going on?'

Dad grabbed Mum's arm to stop her going down the path. Kegan could see his knuckles were white as he squeezed as hard as he could. 'Don't turn your back on me, what's up with him?'

Kegan stood there, fists clenched. The paramedics had said there was no time to waste. A great fountain of anger and fear had come up from his stomach and got stuck in his throat. 'We've got to get going.' His voice shook.

'Please, Mr Wilson.' One put her hand gently on his

father's arm. Kegan flinched. 'We have to get your little boy to hospital as quickly as possible. You can follow in your car.' Strange how everyone assumed you'd got a car.

Dad turned swiftly, angry violence surging in his eyes. 'What's up with him, I said?'

'We're not sure, yet.'

'You're doctors, ain't you?'

They weren't but there wasn't time to explain.

By now, a crowd of neighbours had gathered. Kegan stood there, helpless, hopeless. His dad was kicking up and Gary could be dying.

He lunged forward, punching his father's arm away with all the strength he could find. 'Mum! Tell him to shut-up, we've got to get going!'

His father's fury fell into thin air as the ambulance doors slammed shut and they were on their way. Mum cried noisily in the corner. Kegan watched as the paramedic bent over his brother, adjusting the tiny oxygen mask they'd put over his face. Silent tears fell on to his clasped hands. From the window he glimpsed his father, standing helplessly by the kerb, for once in his life, thankfully, defeated.

Part Two

9

Kegan sat watching the foxes. The cubs were bigger, bolder now, scrapping and rolling. Only Amber wasn't thriving. She sat on her own most of the time, only eating what scraps the others had left. He'd tried to put food to one side for her but the others always got it first. He noticed that sometimes Slink didn't bother with her, washing the others but leaving her to try to clean herself. His heart turned over. He knew what it was like to be the outsider.

A little distance away, the vixen sat watching him. She stared, motionless, the wind kissing her fur. He knew her eyes could see his pain. It seemed he was inside her head, looking out at himself, a pathetic skinny figure in scruffy jeans and top, hair spiky and uncombed, face blotched with crying, mind a pit of sorrow. He could feel her heart beating in sympathy with his. It made him feel a bit better, knowing she understood. She drew her eyes away and looked at her cubs the same way that Mum had looked at Gary when it was already too late.

Too late.

Kegan's knees were drawn up to his chin.

'I'm really sorry,' Zoë had said when she heard. She'd got tears in her eyes even though she hadn't known his little brother. He would have liked to take him to meet her and Anna but had never got the chance. Now it was too late.

Too late.

Her mum, *Mummy*, had written him a letter. The first in his life he'd ever received. *Please let us know if there's anything we can do.* Lots of people had written letters and sent cards to his parents. Teachers from school. People in the street. People they didn't even know. People who'd read about Gary in the papers. But they couldn't do anything. No one could.

Gary was dead.

Dead.

Ashes to ashes . . . dust to dust.

He picked up a stick and began to draw vague patterns in the dust of the scrapyard floor. Whirls and shell-shapes, a house, a face, digging harder, making canyons in the dirt, angrily digging as hard as he could until the stick broke and he flung it as far as he could. He felt tears sting the back of his eyes. The baby had looked so peaceful when all the tubes and wires had been taken out and they had switched off the life support machine. They had covered him up to the chin so you couldn't see the rash on his body or the places where blood had seeped through his skin.

The doctor had sorrow in her eyes when she told them. Meningococcal meningitis. The bacteria had swooped out of the blue. There had been nothing anyone could do.

Home was worse than ever. Mum, chain-smoking, crying all the time, unable to cope. Blaming herself. Kegan did his best. Getting the meals, shopping, cleaning up as best he could. Gran was there a lot. Tight lipped, trying to help but not succeeding. His father was defeated, bitter, somehow shrunken to half his size. He lolled in front of the telly, can in one hand, remote control in the other, staring at the screen but seeing nothing. Fat lot of good he'd been in a crisis. A sad, boozy bully. Kegan wasn't even afraid of him any more.

He didn't care if he ranted and raved or swiped him or threatened to kill him or called him a useless waste of space. Surely nothing worse could ever happen than had happened already? It was all pretty clear. Dad had another reason for hating him now. *He* was alive and Gary wasn't.

Kegan was spending more and more time away from the house. Wandering the streets, sitting in the park pavilion, coming to the scrappies. Anywhere Dad wasn't suited him down to the ground. Anywhere *no one* was, even better.

There were footsteps. Slink sniffed the air as the cubs retreated into the safety of the earth. Then suddenly Zoë was beside him.

'Oh dear, I've scared them away.'

'They'll come back.' He'd wanted to be alone but now she was here he was glad she'd come.

'I've been looking for you.'

'Yeah?'

'I went to the park first but I should have known you'd be here.'

'Yeah.'

'Are you all right?' She sat down, her shoulder touching his.

He shrugged. Everyone was asking that. Teachers, other kids, the school counsellor. The answer was 'no', he wasn't all right. But there wasn't anything anyone could do about it.

What he couldn't understand was that although he had changed, everything else was the same. School, the noise, the Head stomping around like Hitler, Bodger whingeing. Only those who called him Rat-boy now moved silently aside as he walked past. He knew they were wondering if he carried the disease his brother had died of and were scared they might catch it. He couldn't be bothered to tell them he'd had to have injections against it.

Zoë looked at the patterns he'd drawn in the dust. 'They look like a symbol language, you know, like ancient Egyptian hieroglyphics.'

'What?'

She sighed. 'Never mind.' Then she put her hand on his arm. 'Have you forgotten about the builders moving in?'

'No, 'course not.'

Saving the foxes was more important than ever. You'd got to save everything you could. But he'd been too tired and too sad to think about it for a while. Anyway, what could they do?

'They're bound to start digging the place up soon.'

He gazed at her. 'Think so?'

'Mummy read in the paper that they've been wanting to build factories here for years so they're not going to waste time now, are they?'

'No, s'pose not.'

'We've got to do something, Kee.'

'Yeah, but I don't see what.'

'We could move the foxes somewhere else.'

He looked at her scornfully. He thought she'd have come up with something better than that. 'Yeah? How? They're wild animals. They're not going to just let us take them somewhere on collars and leads, are they?'

She looked away, gazing out over the piles of scrapped cars. 'No . . . I don't know. I've been racking my brains like anything.' She turned to look at him again. 'But all I know is that we can't lose Slink and Red and the cubs. Not them as well.'

'As well?'

'As well as Gary.'

He sniffed, retreating back inside himself again. 'No.'

Zoë sighed and sat there with him in a silence that was filled with unspoken words. The cubs were venturing out again. Sniffing the sunshine, blinking in the light. She had a bone for them and a bag of left-overs. She crept forward and scattered them, then came back to be by his side.

Star and Kirk were scrapping over the bone. Kegan rummaged in his bag. For the first time for a while he'd brought his sketch book. Zoë watched as he drew the two cubs, one each end of the bone, tugging and growling, their claws digging in the dirt, their bottoms in the air. Tails waving. His pencil moved over the page swiftly as the animals grew and took life on the paper in front of her eyes.

Amber was watching from the entrance, ready to disappear inside at the first hint of danger.

Slink sat washing her face, the pale tip of her tail swishing, raising little dust storms in the dirt. She looked better, coat sleek and shining, eyes bright. They hadn't seen Red for a while but knew he was still around, marking the area round the earth, warning others to keep away from his territory.

'That's absolutely stunning.' At first he'd hated Zoë seeing him draw but he'd got used to it now. She never said anything until he'd almost finished. She just sat and watched. 'Has Markie Mark talked to you any more about the scholarship?'

'He's given up.'

'No, Kee, *you're* the one who gives up. Remember?'

He stuffed the sketch pad away and turned, anger flaring in his eyes. 'That was a pig thing to say.'

He looked away, the tears pricking again. He wished they would stop but somehow they just wouldn't. They just kept coming and coming. Whenever he got upset or angry, cold or tired or hungry they were always there, threatening to spill.

'Sorry.' She looked sheepish. 'But someone's got to do something about you, Kee.'

'No one's got to do anythin' about me. I'm OK as I am.'

'No, you're not.'

He clenched his jaw together. Suddenly he wanted to be alone again. Alone for ever. Away from worries about the foxes. Away from Zoë telling him what he did or didn't need. He got up, hauling his bag on his shoulder. 'I'm off.'

She got up too. 'Wait, Kee, I'm sorry.'

He turned, angrier still. 'What I do's none of your bloody business. Just leave me alone.' He ran then, away from her, away from Slink and the cubs, away from grief, running, running, wanting to escape from the planet.

At the end of the lane he felt a fool. Why did he keep flaring up for no reason? She had only been trying to help. He turned but she wasn't following. Fatty had yelled at him as he ran past the caravan. Maybe the geezer had stopped Zoë in her tracks? He waited but she still didn't appear. He was just deciding whether to go back or not when she came sauntering coolly through the gates. Not being able to face her he turned and ran again.

At home, Mum had gone to work. Her first night back since Gary died. Dad was in the front room, snoring in front of the telly. Kegan cleared up the kitchen, got himself some tea and took it upstairs. Passing the baby's room he hesitated, then opened the door softly, creeping in as if Gary might still be there, asleep. The cot was still in there, the blankets washed and neatly folded. Someone, some counsellor person who called to see Mum had taken them home to wash. He could smell the unfamiliar smell of fabric softener. The kid hadn't had many toys but what there was had been placed at the end of the cot. A ragged bear, a couple of plastic cars bought from a jumble sale, a torn-up cardboard book, an empty can of Coke he loved to bang with a spoon when Dad wasn't around. Kegan had filed the sharp edge of the hole so he didn't cut himself.

They'd buried his cuddly with him.

Kegan went in and picked up the bear. He held it to his face. He could still smell his brother. Milk. Crisps. Smarties. A faint acid smell that had seemed to be with him everywhere. He carried it into his room. He put the sandwiches on the floor beside the bed and lay down. He cuddled the bear to his chest, drowning it in his ocean of tears.

When he woke up, his head throbbed. It was dark and on the floor the sandwiches were curled and dry. He sat up, wiping the salt from around his eyes. In the distance a train hooted as it thundered over the viaduct. Then he thought he heard Gary cry but knew it couldn't have been him. The house was in silence.

He clicked on the light. Starving, he ate his sandwiches. Then he picked up Gary's bear from where it had fallen on the floor. Under the bed was a tatty cardboard box he kept his precious things in. A few toys he'd had as a kid. Cards from his Gran sent from one of her old people's coach tour holidays. A photo of him and Mum at the seaside when he was little. A book about foxes Zoë had given him. His sketchpad and pencils. And now Gary's bear. He placed it carefully right at the bottom and covered it up so no one would know it was there.

At school he caught up with Zoë in the corridor.

'It's all right,' she said when he said he was sorry. 'I understand.'

'I wish I did,' he said.

'It's going to take time.' She gazed at him. 'You need something else to think about.'

'Yeah? What?'

It was what he wanted most of all. To fill his mind with images that weren't of his brother with all those tubes going in and out and his mother's stricken face and the teddy-bear wreath with 'Gary' in daisy letters, and his dad getting drunk after the funeral and throwing up in the kitchen and Gran yelling at him and calling him names. It had been like some gruesome circus put on for the benefit of everyone but Gary. He knew he would think of it for ever as the day he most wanted to forget but never could.

'The scholarship. The foxes,' Zoë was saying.

'Foxes?' They were in the corridor and Mr Mark had come up beside them. 'Are you still fox mad, Kegan?'

He shrugged. 'Yeah, s'pose so.'

'Of course, he is. Both of us are.' Zoë grabbed Kegan's arm as the teacher went past them towards the art room. 'Come on,' she hissed.

He held back. 'What for?'

'Tell him about the work you've done.'

Mr Mark heard. 'Work?'

Kegan shrugged and shuffled his feet. 'Just the foxes,' he mumbled. 'I've done some studies . . . '

'For the scholarship?'

'Yes,' Zoë said before he'd had a chance to answer.

Kegan threw a dagger at her with his eyes.

'Well?' Mr Mark was waiting.

'Er . . . you could take a look at 'em.' Kegan was still mumbling into his chest. 'If you thought they were good enough . . . '

'Of course they're good enough.' Zoë gazed at Mr Mark, her eyes shining. 'They're extraordinary.'

Mr Mark grinned. 'Bring them in then, lad.'

'Yeah. OK.'

Next day, Mr Mark gazed at them in silence, turning the pages slowly. Once he touched a picture of Star as if he could feel the fur beneath his fingertip.

'That's Amber.' Kegan pointed to a drawing of the tiny cub sitting on her own by the fence. 'She's the runt. See, she's got a funny leg at the front. We were scared she wouldn't survive but she seems to be OK, although she don't grow much.'

Mr Mark still didn't speak even though that was probably the longest sentence he'd ever heard Kegan utter.

Kegan fiddled with the strap of his school bag. His heart sank. They weren't good enough. Why had he let Zoë persuade him? He'd feel a right wally if Markie Mark said they were crap.

At last the teacher looked up. 'Zoë's right. They are extraordinary.'

Kegan heaved a sigh. At least he'd got something right.

'Have you changed your mind about entering?'

'There's no harm in trying I s'pose.'

'I'll help you mount them then all you need to do is fill in a few forms and I'll present them to the board.'

Kegan swallowed. 'Right, thanks.'

'I must warn you, though, I'm putting a couple of others in for it too.'

He shrugged. 'That's OK.'

He stayed behind after school and together he and the art teacher sliced the drawings from the pad and mounted each one on card.

Mr Mark stood back, holding one of the fox family at arm's length. 'Brilliant.'

He put them all in a large folder and tied the top with ribbon. He wrote Kegan's name on a white label stuck to the front. 'There you are, lad. Your portfolio.'

The word sounded good. Portfolio. As if he was a real artist. A someone. A someone whose dreams might come true after all.

'Do you want to take the forms home to fill in?'

He pulled a face. 'Do I have to?'

'Not really. Not if you don't want to.'

'I don't,' Kegan said.

'We could do them at my house.' Zoë had finished her violin lesson and had come in to wait for him.

'Yeah. OK.' To Mr Mark. 'I'll bring 'em back tomorrow.'

Anna was there when they got to Zoë's.

'Kegan, that's wonderful.' She gave him a hug when she heard about him entering for the scholarship. He could smell a faint hospital smell in the hair that tickled his face as she briefly held him close. It reminded him of Gary and he stepped back sharply. Anna smiled at him. 'When will you hear if you've been successful?'

He shrugged. 'Dunno.'

'What do you mean "if"?' Zoë grinned. 'You mean "when".'

Together they filled in the form. There wasn't much to it really. Name, address, date of birth. Parents' names. A place where Mr Mark had already put his signature. At the bottom was a space where Kegan had to write why he would like to be awarded the scholarship. He bit the end of his pen, frowning, stuck for an answer.

Zoë had one as usual. 'Because it will help you escape.'

He gazed at her scornfully. 'I can't put that, even if it's true.'

'OK, then.' She fiddled with her hair. 'Put this. *I would like to be awarded the Jenny Turner scholarship because it will help me to fulfil my dream of one day becoming a professional artist.*'

'Blimey.' He chuckled.

'That sounds good,' Anna said. 'I'd be impressed if someone applying for a job in my department put that on their form.'

'And anyway, it's true, isn't it?' Zoë asked.

'Yeah . . . I suppose so,' he admitted.

'Put it, then.'

So he wrote it on the form. Sitting back, he thought that a month or so ago he would have felt a right wally writing something like that. He grinned at Zoë and Anna. 'Thanks.'

'Right.' Zoë rubbed her hands together. 'That's one problem out of the way.'

10

Kegan woke late. There was a feeling of dread in his stomach. He'd grown used to coming to with darkness inside him even though it was broad daylight.

At first, when Gary died, in that limbo land between sleeping and waking he'd had to think what was making him feel as if all he wanted to do was curl up and die. It didn't take long to realize what it was. He knew the sensation would be there for ever. All he had to do was get used to it.

That day, though, it was there with a real vengeance. Something gruesome was going to happen. He just knew it. He could hear music in his head too, the scary kind of music they play in horror movies. He'd heard it the day the baby got ill. It was a sure sign something was going to happen.

Since Gary, they'd had a phone put in and it rang before he'd even got to the bathroom.

Downstairs he heard his mum answer it, then she called up the stairs. She had just got in from work.

'Kee! It's your girlfriend.'

Zoë! He ran downstairs and grabbed the phone. 'Yeah?'

She sounded out of breath and desperate. 'Kee, we've just driven past the lane, there's lorries everywhere. They've started putting in a new road round the back of the yard. I've made Mummy stop so I can phone you. What are we going to do?'

The feeling of doom had come right up into his throat.

72

'I dunno. Look, get your mum to drop you off and go back to the yard. I'll be there as quick as I can.'

'You're off early.' His dad was reading the paper when he went in to grab a packet of crisps for breakfast. Cigarette smoke curled from behind the pages like signals.

'I'm meeting someone before school.' Kegan took the last packet from the cupboard.

'His girlfriend,' Mum said, dishing a mountain of fried bacon onto Dad's plate. She looked pale and tired, dark circles painted beneath her eyes. She moved like someone in a dream.

'She's not my *girlfriend*, she's just a friend, that's all.'

'That doctor's kid?' Dad said. He didn't look Kegan in the eye.

'Yeah. So what?'

He waited for a caustic remark but his dad just snorted and went back to the *Sun*. Kegan still couldn't get used to his dad backing off.

'I need some bread from the corner shop before you go to school.' Clouds of steam rose as Mum dumped the hot frying pan into a cold bowl of water.

'Why can't *he* go?' A month ago he wouldn't have dared say a thing like that.

'You're joking!' His dad glanced up from the paper.

'Well, you'll have to go without then.' Kegan grabbed his coat and went out, tearing open the crisps and scoffing them as he ran down the path.

At the yard, Zoë had crept in through their secret way. She was watching a JCB loading a lorry with a pile of scrap. A bulldozer was knocking down the fence at the other end of the yard close to where the foxes had their earth. Clouds of dust rose everywhere. The noise was deafening.

When she saw him arrive she ran towards him. She clutched his arms and shouted above the din. 'What are we going to do?'

'I don't know!'

They stood there feeling helpless, hopeless. Kegan imagined the foxes below ground, huddled together, scared of the thunder above their heads, the vibration, the noise as the great machines trundled around moving great piles of scrap and digging deep into the ground. He could hear the panic stricken beats of their hearts, the cries of the cubs as their world fell to pieces around them. He tried to send his thoughts to Slink. Come out! Bring the cubs and run for your lives! But his mind was so blocked with fear there was a brick wall around it.

Zoë began to cry. He put his arm round her awkwardly. She couldn't go to pieces, without her he would do the same.

A man in a white hard-hat appeared.

'What are you kids doing here?'

Zoë wiped her face on her sleeve and was just about to say something when Kegan got a word in first for a change. Maybe if they pleaded with the man he'd keep the bulldozers away?

'There's a family of foxes live 'ere,' he blurted out. 'You've got to be careful or you'll dig up their earth.'

'Foxes!' Hard-hat laughed as if the word was funny. 'They'll scarper when we get too close, don't you worry. Cunning buggers, foxes.'

'But they've got cubs,' Zoë said. 'They're too little to run very fast.'

The man took off his hat and scratched his bald head underneath. 'Well one or two less won't hurt. They're a damn nuisance most of the time. Never mind about the foxes, you kids had better scarper. You're trespassing, you know.'

'We don't care.' Zoë was still crying tears of fury and frustration. She wiped them away angrily. 'Surely you could just avoid this little piece of land. It's not much to ask, is it?'

'I'm not standing here arguing.' The man took a mobile phone from his pocket. 'If you're not gone when I get back I'll get someone to remove you.'

With that he walked away.

'Bloody pig!' Zoë yelled. 'I hope someone comes and digs up your home and kills your children!' Her voice was lost amid the squeals of metal against metal and the rumble of huge tyres in the dirt.

'I'm not going to school.' Kegan sat down. 'I'm staying here. They can run me over if they like.'

'Me too, then.' Zoë said and plonked down beside him.

They had only been there a few minutes when Zoë suddenly nudged his arm. He'd been sitting with his knees drawn up to his chin, surrounded by a dark shroud of misery.

'Kee! There's Red!'

The big dog fox had slipped in through the loose fence panel. A shifting, dappled shadow, emerging from the clouds of dust. He ignored the great machines trundling around barely a hundred metres away, threw a glance at Kegan and Zoë and disappeared underground. Minutes later he reappeared with one of the cubs fastened in his jaws by the scruff of its neck. The cub dangled from Red's mouth as he stood by the entrance waiting.

'Has he killed it?' Kegan's heart thundered a wild beat.

'Don't be a dummy, he's only carrying him.' Zoë drew in her breath. 'It's Star.' The cub was easily recognizable by its dark muzzle and two white socks.

Then Slink came out. She had Kirk by the scruff. She looked around briefly then the two adult foxes slid silently through the fence panel and were gone.

Zoë looked at Kegan. She was smiling and crying at the same time. 'We should have known they would look after their babies. We've been worrying for nothing.'

He realized he'd been holding his breath. 'Where do you think they've taken 'em?'

She shook her head. 'I don't know. But somewhere safe I'm sure. Isn't it simply wonderful?'

'Brilliant.'

'They'll come back for Amber, just you wait.'

So they waited and waited for what seemed like hours. Slink and Red didn't come.

By the time the machines fell silent for the day half the fence had been bulldozed and the site cleared. A gang of workers had started putting up a new boundary. In a day or two that end of the yard would be sealed off and their secret way in would be gone for ever.

Still Slink and Red hadn't returned.

'They can't abandon her.' Zoë sounded desolate. 'She can't look after herself.'

'They're probably scared to come back because of all the machines.'

'Yes.' Zoë sniffed. 'Maybe.'

Kegan sat in silence beside her. The darkness was inside him again. He had a horrible, sinking feeling Slink and Red wouldn't risk coming back to rescue Amber. Sometimes, you were so scared you didn't dare do what you really wanted.

It was twilight when the tiny cub emerged. She sat at the entrance, her tail swishing gently. She gave a little whine and hobbled around listlessly, sniffing and snuffling in the dirt, looking up and around, her eyes

76

scanning. Then she gave three high, childish barks into the night sky.

Kegan strained his ears for a reply but no sound of an answering bark came across the landscape to reassure her.

Amber whined again and lay down, her nose in between her front paws.

'They're never coming.' Zoë was telling him what he already knew. 'What are we going to do?'

'Dunno.'

They waited until the sun had gone down and the moon had climbed the rooftops. Amber had wandered off but came back every now and then. She had never been more than a few metres from the earth in her short life. Eventually, tired and hungry she crawled back down. Kegan imagined her curled there, tail tucked round, alone and cold. He knew exactly how she felt.

He sat with his forehead on his knees. Zoë beside him, silent.

Then she whispered in his ear in a small, sad voice. 'Poor Amber. We just can't allow her to be killed.'

'No, and I ain't leaving until we've thought of something.'

'I'll phone Mummy.' Zoë dragged her mobile from her pocket and switched it on. 'She might have an idea.'

He listened while she explained.

'No, we haven't been to school,' he heard her say. 'Did they phone to ask where I was?'

She listened while her mother spoke.

'But we couldn't go and leave Amber to be killed, could we? Yes, I'm sorry but we just couldn't.'

She listened for a while. 'Oh, do you think they would? Yes. Very well. No, we're going to stay here, I told you, we're not going to leave her. Oh, yes, all right.'

When she powered down the phone she had a grin on her face. 'Mummy says we should phone the RSPCA. She thinks they might try to dig her out and take her somewhere safe.'

'Yeah? When?'

'In the morning. She said we should wait a while. Slink still might come back, when everything's quiet.'

'Yeah.' He doubted it though. 'Was she angry you bunked off school?'

'Not really,' Zoe said. 'She knows it was in a good cause. She's bringing us some soup and sandwiches and blankets so we can stay all night.' She held out the phone. 'Do you want to phone your mum?'

He shook his head. 'Nah. She'll be at work and the old man won't notice whether I'm there or not or care if I bunked off. How will your mum get in?'

'I'll go round the front and meet her.'

It seemed hours before they returned. He sat facing the fence. He could hear his own breaths above the distant roar of the traffic. Once, he crawled across and put his ear to the ground to find out if he could hear the little fox breathing or moving about. He saw her in his mind's eye. Curled and sad. He wished she knew they were going to make sure she was saved.

Half an hour later Zoë appeared back with Anna armed with a rucksack full of food and three sleeping bags. Anna was dressed in combat trousers, boots, and fleecy jacket. Her hair tied up with a scarf. She looked about nineteen. Kegan thought of his own mum, tired and scarred by the turmoil of her life. Anna had been the same once, Zoë said, when Zoë's father died. Maybe when the fox was safe, when he'd heard about the scholarship, he'd try to persuade Mum to get a decent job somewhere. Somewhere where she could work in the daytime and go out with friends in the evening. Maybe there would be a job at the hospital? Mum had admired the nurses who had cared for Gary. Anna would help he felt sure. He made up his mind to ask.

'I'm not sure I should be doing this.' Anna dumped the stuff beside him. 'We must all be stark, raving mad. You know we're trespassing, don't you?'

'We don't care.' Zoë ripped the lid off the sandwich box. 'We don't care about anything as long as Amber is saved.'

'Tell that to the judge,' Anna said and grinned.

'Why do you think they haven't come back?' Zoë asked when they'd eaten and tucked themselves into the sleeping bags to keep warm.

'It could be because they're too scared. And she's the runt of the litter,' Anna said. 'In the animal kingdom I'm afraid it's the survival of the fittest.'

'And in the human kingdom,' Kegan said.

They both stared at him but didn't answer.

'Supposing we doze off and they come for her while we're asleep?' Anna said.

'We'll make sure one of us is awake the whole time.' Zoë snuggled up to her mother. 'I'll stay awake first, if you like. You get some sleep, you two.'

But he couldn't. However hard he tried his mind kept whirling round and round.

Kegan didn't think he would ever forget that night spent under the stars with Zoë and Anna. It was a chilly, clear night with the sky a blizzard of stars. The sounds of the city seemed magnified a hundred times. Once he looked up and saw the red and green lights of an aeroplane skimming across the sky. He wondered where it had been or where it was going and if he would ever get to go on one if he became a famous artist. He smiled to himself. He was getting as bad as Zoë. But

79

dreams didn't hurt anyone, it was only when they failed to come true that you'd be sorry you ever had them.

Still, Slink and Red didn't return.

He was aware of Anna and Zoë talking in low voices. He'd got no idea two people could find so much to say to one another.

Zoë squirmed inside her sleeping bag. 'I'm never going to get any sleep. I wish morning would come so we can rescue her. What time will you phone, Mummy?'

'Early.' Anna shivered. 'I must be mad,' was the last thing Kegan heard her mutter as he finally drifted into an uncomfortable and restless doze.

He came to just before dawn. He lay still, listening to the distant rumble of traffic, aware he'd been dreaming a dream of saving fox cubs. Then a blackbird began singing somewhere, its voice echoing above the distant sounds. The tumbling notes seemed to rise up and disappear into the morning air. Beside him, Zoë was wide awake watching the sun creeping up over the rooftops. They were outlined in black, silhouettes against the red of the dawn sky.

'You awake?' she asked as he stirred, trying to get the stiffness out of his legs.

'Wasn't asleep,' he muttered, ashamed he'd been comfortable enough to doze off.

'Yes, you were,' she argued. 'You were snoring like a pig.'

'Rubbish.' He couldn't bear the thought.

'Well.' She grinned. 'Just a little snort now and then.'

He thought of his dad and the sound of his snores rumbling through the thin walls of Kegan's bedroom. He had never known how Mum could sleep through such a din. He wondered vaguely if they'd missed him.

'Any sign of Slink or Red?'

She shook her head. 'No.'

Anna stirred. 'God, I've been asleep!'

'It's all right, Mummy, I've been awake.'

'Good job someone was,' Kegan muttered.

The RSPCA inspectors turned up half an hour after Anna phoned.

Kegan heaved a sigh of relief when he saw the inspectors coming across the yard towards them with a puzzled looking building foreman. It was the one who'd spoken to them yesterday. One of the inspectors was carrying a large wire cage, the other a spade.

'You kids still here?' The foreman frowned then noticed Anna wasn't a kid at all. 'These yours?' he asked.

'Yes,' she said before Kegan could say he wasn't. In fact, when he thought about it, he didn't really feel as if he was anyone's. 'I'm sorry,' Anna went on. 'But they're absolutely determined to save this animal so it's no use arguing.'

The inspectors introduced themselves and listened while they explained what had happened.

'Right, you two,' one called Liz said. 'Shouldn't be a problem. You're absolutely sure the parents aren't coming back?'

'It's been a whole day,' Kegan told them.

'And we've got to move into this area today,' the foreman said.

'Right, show us where the little fella is then.'

'We think it's a she,' Zoë piped up. 'Because she's so small. She's lame so she can't even run away.'

'She trusts us,' Kegan said. 'She knows we won't let them kill her.'

'We wouldn't have done it on purpose.' The foreman took off his hat and scratched his bald head. 'You can't stop a huge project like this for a flipping fox.'

'Why not?' Zoë stared at him hard until he looked away.

Kegan saw the two RSPCA inspectors grin as the foreman went away mumbling and shaking his head.

'We'd all better stand round in case she makes a bolt for it,' John, the other inspector, said.

They stood in a tight circle as the spade went in, deeper and deeper.

Kegan suddenly realized he was holding his breath.

'Please, be careful.' Zoë was on tenterhooks. 'You might hurt her.'

Then, there Amber was, cringing away from the spade, curled up and scared stiff, her eyes wide and full of fear.

Suddenly she made a bolt for it but Kegan was there, bending and scooping her gently up from the hollow.

'Careful,' Liz warned. 'She could give you a nasty bite.' She had already put on a pair of canvas gloves but it was too late, Kegan had Amber.

Safe.

The young fox struggled violently, yelping, trying to bite his hands but he held her firmly under his arm, one hand stroking her head.

'Hold her by the scruff,' Liz said.

'It's OK,' he was murmuring softly. He'd dreamed of holding her, feeling her fur, her fragile bones in his hands. 'You're safe now.' As if she understood, the cub suddenly relaxed and allowed him to run his fingers over her back and her tail. Her fur was soft, just as he'd imagined. He could feel how thin and cold she was and his heart turned. He'd had a dream they would save her and now it had come true. Zoë was right. *Sometimes* they did.

He suddenly realized they were all staring at him, listening to his soft words. He saw Anna swallow and knew she and Zoë had felt the magic too.

Zoë had tears in her eyes as she came and touched

Amber's coat. 'It's all right, now,' she murmured too. 'We're going to make sure you'll be all right.'

'Put her in here.' Liz picked up the cage and held it open. Amber struggled violently again. Kegan didn't know if she didn't want to go in the cage or if she didn't want to leave the safety of his arms.

Liz was waiting. 'Put her in,' she said again and nodded.

He stroked the cub's head, calming her as he placed her inside. Liz put the cage down and snapped the door shut. The cub turned in circles, scratching and biting at the wire. Then she stopped as if she knew it was hopeless. She looked up through the top, staring at them. Her nostrils flared, trying to catch the scent of the freedom she had lost.

Kegan bent. 'It's OK,' he repeated. 'You're safe.'

She gazed at him with an unblinking stare then crouched down, ready to flee even though there was nowhere to go.

'That's brilliant.' Zoë knelt down beside Kegan. 'We must get her something to eat. She'll be starving hungry.'

'She'll be too upset to eat for a while,' Liz told them. 'We'll take her to the animal hospital to get her checked over.'

'Then what?' Anna asked.

'We could take her to the sanctuary where Rudolph went,' Zoë suggested.

As they walked back through the yard to the RSPCA van Anna explained about the sanctuary.

'But she's wild,' Kegan protested. 'She doesn't want to be shut up in a cage all her life.'

'They're not in cages.' John already knew about the place. 'They have big runs and earths just as they do in the wild. But you're right, son, this little one should be released.'

'But she's too little to look after herself,' Zoë insisted. 'And she's got that deformed leg.' She gazed up at the man. 'What do you think's best for her?'

'Well,' he said. 'She would have stayed with the family group until the autumn so that's where she would be best off.'

'Sometimes females stay with the parents until they're old enough to breed,' Liz added.

'Yeah.' Kegan remembered what he had read in the book Zoë gave him. 'It's the dog foxes that go off on their own to find a new mate.'

John put the cage into the back of the van. Amber crouched there, staring at them all. 'She's quite strong for a runt, even though she's small and thin. I reckon she would survive in the wild.' But then he shook his head. 'Although without family support . . . '

'I know.' Kegan had been thinking, his mind spinning crazily to try to find a solution. 'We'll find Slink and Red and give her back to them. They wouldn't have deserted her on purpose. Wherever they've gone they're thinking about her and wishing they were brave enough to come back.'

They all stared at him. He went red and shuffled his feet, amazed at the long speech he'd just made.

'They could be miles away,' Anna said.

He shook his head. He knew they wouldn't go far. 'No. This is their territory,' he insisted. 'They'll stay around here until the family splits up.' He gazed at Zoë, his eyes shining. 'We can do it, Zo. Remember what you said about making your dreams come true? We can find 'em, I know we can.'

She grinned suddenly. 'Oh, Kee, you're brilliant and wonderful.' He thought for one horrible minute she was going to throw her arms around him but instead she turned to Liz and John. 'Will they keep her at the hospital until we've found her parents? I'll pay for her keep out of my allowance.'

Liz smiled. 'Yes, I'm sure they will if they've got room. But you haven't got a snowball's chance in hell of—'

'Yes, we have.' Zoë wasn't having any of that. She turned to Kegan. 'Where shall we start?'

11

'We'll try to track them,' Kegan said when they had watched the van drive through the gates and down the lane with Amber inside.

Anna glanced at her watch. 'I'm on duty at two,' she said. 'I've really got to get home.'

'That's all right, Mummy.' Zoë gave her a hug. 'Thank you so much for all your help.'

'Yeah,' Kegan mumbled. 'Ta.'

Anna took some money out of her pocket. 'Buy yourselves some breakfast and for goodness' sake be careful. And don't go near the railway line.' It was the first time Kegan had heard her tell Zoë not to do something.

'We'll be careful, honestly.' Zoë hugged her again. 'I love you.'

Anna held her at arm's length. 'You know you might never locate them?'

Zoë shook her head. 'We shall,' she said. 'I know we shall.'

Anna sighed and got into the four-wheel drive. They watched her drive away.

'Breakfast first?' Zoë asked.

'If we're quick.'

They discussed strategy over bacon and eggs at the little café next to the corner shop.

'They would have gone to the nearest safe place, I reckon.'

'Away from the noise of the machines,' Zoë said.

'Right. We'll go back through the fence and try to track them along the bank.' Kegan could already see Slink in his mind's eye. Hiding in a derelict house or under someone's shed, in the old railway goods yard. Anywhere where they would be safe.

'I'm sure you should have phoned your mum,' Zoë said as they tramped back into the yard and out through the fence where they had last seen the foxes.

He shrugged. 'Na, she'll think I've been in and gone out again. And I told you, my dad won't notice.'

'How can he not notice you've been gone so long?'

Sometimes he got cheesed off with her not understanding. 'Easy. Anyway I've told you a million times. He reckons I'm a waste of space.'

Zoë bent down at something lying on the ground. 'Look! Fox spraint.'

'What?'

'Spraint. It's what you call fox droppings. It's how they mark their territory.'

'I know that, stupid. I just didn't know it was called that.'

'It means Slink has passed this way.'

'It could be from another fox.'

Zoë shook her head. 'No, you said yourself this is their territory. Come on, let's see if there's any more.'

She ran down the bank, across the ditch and up the other side. The narrow road flanked a row of walled back gardens. A man was walking his terrier.

'Do you ever see any foxes around here?' Zoë bent to stroke the terrier. He showed his teeth at her then rolled on his back for her to tickle his stomach. Kegan was amazed how she could speak to someone she'd never met before without feeling a wally.

'A few,' the man said. 'Most people think they're a

pest but I like to see them. Ben here goes mad when he smells them.'

Zoë rubbed the terrier's stomach. 'We've been studying a family that lived in the old scrapyard.'

'Eyesore that place,' the man commented.

Kegan didn't like to say it was his favourite place in the universe.

'They're clearing some of it,' Zoë rambled on. 'And the machines have scared away our foxes. We're trying to track them down.'

'Good luck.' The man yanked the terrier to his feet. 'Come on, Ben, that's enough.'

'Have you got any idea where they might . . . ?' Zoë called out but the man had lost interest and walked off down the street with the terrier pulling at the lead. 'Oh, well,' she sighed. 'Never mind.'

There was a woman carrying a bulging supermarket carrier in each hand. Kegan hung back while Zoë ran to catch her up.

'Excuse me,' Zoë said. 'Have you seen any foxes around here lately?'

The woman gazed at her as if she was mad running up behind her and asking a question out of the blue. 'Foxes? Oh . . . er . . . yes. They raid the bins all the time.'

'Have you seen any with cubs?'

'Cubs?' she repeated as if to reassure herself of the question. She shook her head. 'No.'

'Thank you so much,' Zoë said and danced back to him. She told him what the woman had said.

'It's no use asking about cubs,' he said. 'They'd still be hiding them somewhere.'

Further along, the narrow street came to a dead end. A high concrete wall separated it from the old goods yard.

They stood there looking up.

'They'd never get over that.' Kegan shook his head.

'No.' Zoë had walked backwards into the road, her eyes searching up and down. 'But there's an old gate down there. Let's go and look.' She began to run along the side of the wall. 'Come on, Kee, what are you waiting for?'

He sprinted after her, avoiding the rubbish, drink cans, fish and chip wrappers, bags of garbage that littered the place. Zoë was jumping over brambles and undergrowth that in places hugged the wall almost to its top.

Panting, they came to a halt. A long disused road ended in a pair of metal gates half strangled by weeds and brambles.

'Do you think they could get through all this?' Zoë stood by his side.

Then Kegan noticed a place where the brambles had been trampled. There was a narrow tunnel that went right between the bars of the gate. He bent and picked off a strand of red fur.

'Fox!' Zoë breathed. 'Or a ginger cat.' They had seen several wild looking moggies haunting the perimeter of the yard.

Kegan peered through. There was a definite path worn on the other side.

'Here,' he said.

She bent beside him, shaking her head. 'It doesn't look big enough for foxes.'

But he had seen a picture in his fox book. A large dog fox, as big as Red, pushing his way through a hole in a fence that looked hardly wide enough for a rat. 'It's big enough for *them* but how do *we* get through?'

'We need a ladder.' Zoë was still staring at the gates as if she hoped they would open as if by magic.

'Don't be daft.'

She turned to him, hands on hips. 'All right then, shall we fly over?'

He was thinking. 'If we clear all this stuff away I reckon we could squeeze between the bars.'

And by the time they had kicked and tugged at the weeds and fetched sticks to bash down the brambles they could see he was right.

Zoë went first, squeezing her slender body sideways between the bars, breathing in, getting her head stuck but twisting it one way and another until, red faced, she was through.

For the first time in his life Kegan was glad he was skinny.

'Blimey,' he said. 'That was bloomin' painful.'

She grinned, standing knee deep in brambles. Her face was dirty, her hands a pattern of oozing scratches. His too.

He bent to examine the ground. She hunkered down beside him. They stared then looked at one another. 'Droppings,' they both said and laughed.

'Spraint,' he said. Taking the lead now, sure they were on the trail, he forged ahead. 'Come on!' He had a feeling this was going to be one of his better days.

They followed the track, winding through heaps of discarded and rusted machinery, tripping several times on bits of broken metal hidden amongst the weeds.

Through it, they stood by an old workmen's hut and gazed out across the abandoned yard. The rails were rusted, damaged in places, lying higgledy-piggledy. A couple of long-disused goods wagons stood near the entrance to a derelict workshop.

Kegan let out his breath. 'This is as good as the scrappies.'

Zoë grinned. 'You'll be able to come here to draw.'

'Yeah.'

She looked at him then burst out into giggles. 'You look a perfect wreck.'

'Thanks,' he grinned. 'So do you.'

'So.' She had her hands on her hips. 'What now?'

'We look for more signs.'

They walked up and down, eyes glued to the ground until Zoë suddenly exclaimed, 'Look, more droppings.'

'Great,' he said.

There were other fox signs too. Torn up McDonald's boxes, old food cartons dragged from someone's bin. A yoghurt carton with teeth marks where an animal had carried it there.

'I don't reckon any people have been here for years.' He felt a sudden surge of hope. 'It must be foxes.'

'But are they *our* foxes? We're quite a way from the scrapyard.'

He shrugged. 'Who knows?'

'Let's sit and watch, maybe we'll spot them.'

'Right.'

'I wish we'd brought some food,' Zoë said an hour later. It was already gone midday and there hadn't been a sign of any foxes. 'I'm ravenous.'

'Grub for us or for the foxes?'

'Both.'

He sat on a sleeper, his arms round his knees. He thought of all the time he'd spent at the scrappies pretending he was in another world, alien to everyone else, but home to him. It had been different since Zoë. She'd shown him what it was like to share things. Maybe he wouldn't ever go back to the scrappies now the foxes had gone. Maybe he would come here instead. Or maybe he wouldn't need any more to go anywhere alone.

Out of the blue, a picture of Gary came crashing into his head and he suddenly realized hours had gone since he last thought about his brother. The longest time ever since he'd died. He'd planned to show the kid all his favourite places when he'd been old enough. They could have had a great time together playing games and stuff. He remembered thinking he couldn't wait for Gary to grow up. Now he'd have to wait for ever.

He heard Zoë's stomach rumble.

'Do you want to go home? I don't mind staying . . . '

'Don't be a silly boy,' she said. 'This mission belongs to us both.'

They sat a while longer.

'We'd be pretty lucky to find them first time,' he mumbled. He was beginning to think his optimism had been a figment of his wild imagination.

She stood up. 'Let's go down the track a bit, there's lots of derelict buildings and stuff . . . '

They walked towards the old workshops. Then suddenly a strong, dark smell wafted across Kegan's nostrils. The unmistakable smell of a fox.

He clutched her arm, bringing her up sharply. 'Did you smell it?'

She sniffed, then turned, her eyes shining. 'Foxes,' she breathed.

'Let's wait, they're bound to be scared stiff and won't come out if they hear us.'

They waited but nothing moved. There was an uncanny stillness over the old goods yard, as if it was completely isolated from any other part of the town. In the distance traffic roared, overhead a jet's engines whined but here, everything was silent except for their beating hearts.

Then Zoë's mobile phone rang and broke the spell.

It was Anna.

'Yes, we're fine. No, not yet. We will. Bye, Mummy.' Zoë sighed as she switched it off.

'I think we should go back and get some grub for 'em,' Kegan said. 'If they're here they'll smell it and come out.'

'All right,' Zoë said. 'Come home with me.'

He shook his head. 'I'd better get back, I'll meet you later.'

He left Zoë at the bus stop and jogged home.

Indoors, his mum was on the phone. He was surprised to see her, assuming she'd be sleeping after her Friday night shift.

As he walked in she turned and he could see something was wrong. Her eyes were red with crying and it didn't look as if she'd combed her hair for a week. His heart sank. She'd been a bit better lately and now seemed back to square one.

'It's all right, Dawn, he's here!' She slammed down the phone.

He dodged as she ran towards him, hurtling down the hallway as if being blown by a hurricane. It looked as if he was really in for it.

But he couldn't get away as she grabbed him. He put his hands over his head to protect himself from her blows. It was stupid really, he was taller than she was and probably a lot stronger. She was yelling. 'Brian! He's here!'

Oh God, he thought, she's getting Dad, now I'm *really* in for it.

But she wasn't raining blows on his head as he'd expected. She'd put her arms round him and was hugging him and crying. 'Oh, Kee, where've you been?' And even when Dad hauled himself off the settee and came through the door he didn't rant on about making a row and what had Kegan been up to and he deserved a good hiding. He stood there watching the two of them, his mouth open to yell but nothing coming out. Speechless and helpless in the face of any kind of emotion that wasn't anger.

Kegan stood with his arms at his sides, letting her hug him as she hadn't done since he was little. He could feel her heart beating against him.

At last she held him at arm's length. 'For God's sake, Kee!' She sniffed and wiped her tears with the palm of her hand. 'We've been going spare.'

'Sorry.'

'But where've you been?'

He swallowed back his own tears and shrugged. 'Out.'

His dad found his tongue, came closer, flicking the ash from his cigarette on to the floor. 'Out where?'

'Just out.'

Mum linked her arm through his and led him away from his father's confusion and into the kitchen. Gran was there, drying the dishes.

'Well, you're a fine one,' she said, turning round to stare at him. 'And you look a right mess, what have you been up to?'

'Nothing much,' he said.

She pulled a face. 'Don't look like it.'

'You'd better tell us,' his dad threatened from the doorway.

'Leave him alone, Brian,' Gran said. 'He's home, isn't he, what more do you want? You'd better phone the police and tell them he's back.'

'The police?' Kegan turned to his mum. 'What've they got to do with anything?'

'We phoned them because you've been out all night. Didn't you think we'd be worried?' His mother's hand shook slightly as she lit a cigarette from a packet on the table.

He shrugged, not liking to say he didn't think they'd even notice. He sat down and fiddled with a lipstick-stained butt in the overflowing ashtray. 'Sorry.'

'Is that all you can say?' Gran had finished drying up. She came to sit beside him, peering at him closely. 'Your mum's been going bananas.'

'Sorry,' he said again, not looking at her.

He heard his mother sigh as she stood close behind him as if to stop him pushing his chair back and escaping again. 'Well, it don't matter where you've been, I suppose. The main thing is you're OK.' She put a hand on his shoulder. 'I thought we'd lost you too.'

He stood up and turned to face her. 'Sorry.' He put his arms round her. Out of the corner of his eye he saw his dad turn and go back to the sitting room and slam the door.

Gran shook her head and sighed.

'My mum's never done that before,' he said to Zoë later when they were on their way back to the goods yard. He felt a wally, telling her, but he'd got to tell someone and she was the only one. 'Not since I was a little kid anyway. I thought she stopped loving me once I got bigger.'

'You're such a silly,' she said. 'Everyone's mother loves them.'

'No,' he said. 'Not everyone's. You live in a dream world.'

'Well, most do.' She wouldn't give in. 'It's just that not everyone can show it. Just because they don't say it every five minutes doesn't mean to say it's not true.'

'Yeah,' he said. 'OK. You do, though. You and your mum are always saying it.'

She shrugged. 'Yes, that's true. But not everyone's like us, are they?'

'No,' he said, grinning. 'They definitely ain't.'

Zoë had brought a cooked chicken from the supermarket. The smell made his mouth water.

'This will bring them out.' She unwrapped it and placed it near the spot where they had smelled the fox-smell.

'If it don't,' he said. 'Nothing will.'

They sat some way back. Waiting. Zoë had brought a rucksack with sandwiches and cans of Coke and they sat scoffing, making as little noise as possible.

The light was beginning to fade by the time the first fox appeared. First of all a black muzzle, then two eyes peering warily round from the dark doorway of the old workshop. Nostrils caught the scent of the chicken and the animal came out. A large dog fox, head high, senses alert for danger, tail brushing the ground. It sniffed the air then stepped daintily over the old rails and came towards them.

Kegan heard Zoë draw in her breath. 'It's Red,' she hissed but he was too stunned by their good luck to answer.

Then, as if Red had called to them, the others came out. The cubs first, tumbling over one another to get to the carcass. Then Slink trotting towards them. She watched as the cubs began tearing the chicken apart. She walked the perimeter of their feast, then at last dived in to grab a morsel for herself. Red sat, tail swishing, watching for danger. Once, Kegan caught his eye and the animal stared, one ear twitching, right into his head. Kegan knew the fox could see his thoughts.

Beside Kegan, Zoë had clutched his arm. He could feel her excitement through her fingertips. 'I can't believe it,' she whispered.

'You've got to,' he said. 'Because it's true.'

They waited until the carcass had been devoured then

watched as the cubs played and scrapped, rolling and growling in the grass that grew between the rails. Slink and Red sat washing themselves, then the family moved off to another part of the yard and disappeared out of sight.

'Brilliant,' Zoë breathed.

On the way back, they made plans.

'We'll go to the animal hospital tomorrow and fetch Amber,' Zoë said. She did a little skip. 'It's going to be wonderful when the family are all back together.'

'Yeah,' he said. 'Great.' There must have been something in his voice that made her look at him sharply.

'You sounded sad then.'

He shrugged, not knowing how she always noticed. 'I was thinking about Gary,' he admitted. 'We won't ever be back together again.'

She fiddled with her fingernail. 'Like us,' she said. 'Daddy won't ever be with us again, either.'

'No.'

She gazed at him, her eyes bright in the light from the overhead lamps that lit the narrow street. 'Mummy said he'll always be in our hearts.'

'Yeah.' He swallowed.

'And Gary will always be in yours.'

'Yeah,' he said again.

That night he dreamed of Slink. She was crouched in the corner of a dark building. The moonlight shone through jagged, broken panes of glass. She had been suckling the cubs but now they were fast asleep, curled together in a knot of fur and whiskers. In the other corner Red was asleep, oblivious to her uneasiness. She got up and went out, padding silently across a derelict landscape. She made her way through a gate and skirted a line of garden walls then across a road to where a fence used to be. She sniffed around, her ears and eyes alert for danger. Once a car thundered past and she crouched against a row of dustbins. Then she ran on, her heart pounding as she encountered huge machines and the strong smell of man. When she came to the place where her cubs had been born she stopped, gazing round in confusion. She pawed at the ground, scraping the soil up into a mound. She ran round in circles then sat and gave a high, desperate bark. She cocked her ears to listen but when no reply came she turned and ran back the way she had come.

When Kegan awoke he knew she had been telling him what she wanted him to do.

12

He was at Zoë's early.

'I've phoned the animal hospital,' she told him as she opened the door to his knock. 'They're checking with Liz and John and said we can go right over.'

'Great. 'ow do we get there?'

'Mummy's taking us. She's in the shower but she'll be down in a minute.'

Zoë made him some toast, then Anna appeared smelling of herbs and shampoo and drying her hair on a snowy white towel.

Zoë made her eat her breakfast on the way to the hospital. He had never seen anyone drive and eat toast at the same time.

Zoë bounced up and down in the front seat as they drove through the gates. 'I'm longing to see Amber, aren't you?'

'Yeah.' He hadn't had a chance to tell her about his dream.

The cub was in a large pen in a room at the back.

'We've checked her over and got rid of her fleas,' the assistant told them. 'She's a bit underweight but seems fine otherwise. Where did you find her?'

'We didn't *find* her.' Zoë looked indignant. 'We *rescued* her from some beastly men who were going to kill her.'

'Not on purpose,' came a voice behind them and they

turned to see Liz. 'They had to dig up the earth she was hiding in,' she explained to the assistant.

'Well, she *would* have died,' Zoë insisted. 'She would have run off in a panic under the wheels of one of their great machines.'

Kegan was busy staring through the bars of the wire cage. Amber paced up and down, turning her body this way and that but never taking her eyes from him. 'It's OK,' he whispered. 'We're taking you home.'

When Liz spoke again her voice was full of admiration. 'How did you track the parents down?'

He shrugged. 'Luck.'

'Nonsense.' Zoë was grinning. 'We used our skills as wildlife enthusiasts.'

'Yeah.' Kegan grinned too. 'Like I said. Luck.'

When John arrived they put Amber into the back of the van. She went wild, biting at the bars of the cage.

'She's a tough little thing.' John closed the van doors. 'A survivor.'

'Hope so.' Kegan peered through the back windscreen. Amber was crouched, looking up desperately at the light from the window.

'Come with me if you like,' John said to Kegan.

He looked at Zoë. 'Go ahead,' she said. 'Liz can come with Mummy and me and we'll follow you.'

They had already explained about the goods yard and having to squeeze through the gate.

'We'll go round the front,' John said. 'There's another entrance into that yard. We had to go there once when a swan had flown into the overhead power lines.'

When they got there Kegan said, 'Can me and Zoë take her on our own? Slink and Red'll be scared if we all go. They might scarper.'

The two inspectors exchanged glances. 'OK,' Liz said. 'We'll wait here.'

The cage was so large they had to carry it between them. Amber lay on the blanket on the bottom. Not moving but just staring up at them. It was as if she knew she was going on an important journey. They carried her sideways, holding a handle each. They stepped carefully over the old rails and skirted round the edge of the workshops.

By the door, they stopped and put the cage down.

'We've got to wait until Slink comes out.' Zoë rubbed her arms where the cage had been heavy. 'We've got to make sure she knows Amber is here. If we open the door Amber might bolt.'

'Slink will know all right.' Kegan walked back to the place where they had sat before.

Zoë bent down to the cage and he could hear her talking to the cub. He imagined she was saying goodbye. Then she joined him and they sat there waiting. Time seemed to be holding its breath. Kegan felt as if the whole world was waiting for something to happen.

The cub roamed round and round the cage giving little growls and grunts. Then she gave a high bark, then another and another.

'She's saying "Mummy come and get me".' Zoë was sitting with her chin on her knees.

'Not, "why did you leave me"?' Kegan sat beside her, his heart right up in his throat. Supposing the vixen didn't come out? Supposing when he'd seen her in his dream he had just been wishing that Slink would go back to the earth to find her and it hadn't really happened at all?

But then the vixen did come out. She was on her own. When Amber saw her, the cub began crying and pawing at the wire cage. Slink sniffed the bars then started desperately licking the tiny muzzle as Amber tried frantically to push her way through.

101

In a flash, Kegan was up, running towards them. He tried to make his footfalls as soft as possible, almost on tiptoe. As he approached, Slink drew back into the shadows of the doorway but he knew she was there, watching his every move. She knew he had seen her in his dream and had brought her cub back to her.

Swiftly, he undid the clasp on the cage and swung the door outwards. He stepped back away from it, away from the cub, away from the doorway, scooting backwards to the place where Zoë waited. She was on her feet, clutching him as he bumped into her.

The cub had hurtled forward, meeting her mother halfway through the door. Slink rubbed her face against Amber's as if marking her for her own. They both made tiny, yelping sounds of happiness. Then both foxes melted into the shadows of the doorway and disappeared.

Zoë was clutching his arm, her fingers digging into his flesh.

'Hey,' he said. 'You're hurting.'

Her eyes were shining as she looked at him. 'Kee, wasn't that the most wonderful thing you've ever seen in your whole life?'

'Yeah.' He prised her fingers from his arm. 'Certainly was.'

'Come on,' she urged. 'I can't wait to tell Mummy.'

They rescued the cage and carried it back to the gates.

Zoë left him to haul it on his own for the last few metres as she ran and threw herself into Anna's arms. 'Oh, Mummy, you should have seen them. Slink was *so* pleased to see Amber.'

Over the top of her head, Anna smiled at Kegan. 'Well done,' she said. 'Brilliant.'

On the way back, John said, 'You've got a way with

animals by the looks of it, son. Ever thought about working with them when you leave school?'

Kegan shook his head. 'Nope. I'm going to be an artist.'

John grinned. 'You'll just draw them, then, will you?'

'Yeah,' Kegan said. Surprising himself he went on to tell John about the fox studies he'd done and how he'd entered them for the scholarship.

'Good luck.' John shook his hand as he dropped him off.

Kegan grinned. 'Ta. You too.'

'Will you tell your mother what we've done?' Zoë asked when he had joined Anna and Zoë and they had dropped him outside his house.

He shrugged. 'Might do.'

Going in, he decided that's exactly what he *would* do. He would *make* her listen.

She was in the front room watching the lunchtime news and waiting for the latest episode of her favourite daytime Sunday soap.

She looked up as he came into the room. 'You went off early. What you been up to?'

So he sat beside her and told her. Even when her programme came on she didn't tell him to shut-up.

'Blimey, Kee,' she said when he'd finished. 'I dunno, what will you kids get up to next? Rescuing a bloomin' fox.'

Then he told her about the scholarship.

She sat for a minute, staring at the screen. 'Think you'll get it, then?'

He shrugged. 'Dunno. Zoë reckons I will.'

'And your teacher, what's-'is-name?'

'Mr Mark.'

'He thinks you'll get it?'

He shrugged again. 'He wouldn't have put me in for it if he didn't, would he?'

His mother shook her head. 'I don't know, Kee. Why didn't you tell me before?'

'I tried. You didn't listen.'

She stared at him. 'I don't remember.'

He grinned. 'No . . . well . . . you wouldn't, would you.'

'Well.' She picked up the remote and turned the sound up. 'If you get offered it, mind you take it. You'll never get another chance.'

'No,' he said. 'You're right. But what about Dad? He thinks art's crap.'

She gazed at him and he could see her face was filled with a new determination. 'Don't you worry about 'im. Me and your gran will deal with him. And if he don't like it, he can lump it.'

Kegan grinned again. 'Thanks.'

A few weeks later, out of the blue, a letter came from school. Kegan was just coming down the stairs when the post thumped down from the letter box. The one addressed to him was in the middle of the usual junk mail and a couple of red demands for unpaid bills.

He took the mail into the kitchen. His mother had just got home from work and was making herself a cup of tea. His heart pounded like a rock band in his chest as he held his letter up towards her. It had got to be about the scholarship. Mr Mark had told him the administration board would write to him. Supposing he hadn't got it? He suddenly saw an image of Zoë, grinning and nodding at him, her beaded hair dancing round her face. If it hadn't been for her he'd never have been brave enough to go in for it. If he didn't get it he'd be letting her down. And old Markie Mark, Anna, Gran, and now Mum. His courage almost failed as the letter began to burn into the skin of his fingertips.

'What's that?' Mum peered at his envelope after she had flicked briefly through the rest of the mail and tossed it to one side.

He swallowed. 'I think it's about the scholarship.'

She looked at him. 'Oh, blimey. Open it then.'

His fingers trembled as he tore the envelope open. He had heard his father coming down the stairs and was aware of him standing in the doorway, watching and listening.

He took out the letter and read it.

He swallowed and the vibration of his heart's beat seemed to almost knock him sideways.

Then a big grin spread across his face and he suddenly felt he was flying, way up in the sky, as free as a bird, as free as Amber when they'd released her from the cage.

When he looked at Mum there were tears in her eyes.

'You got it,' she said.

He shrugged. 'Yeah. I got it.'

'Art!' His father snorted, turned and went out.

'Don't worry,' Mum said. 'He'll come round.'

She looked at him and grinned and suddenly they both burst out laughing, so hard he thought they would never be able to stop.

Other books by Sue Welford

Nowhere to Run

ISBN 0 19 271818 5

The worst thing that could ever happen had happened. I wanted to run and run. Out of the house, out of the world.

A few drunken moments at a party and Cass's world is turned upside-down. She has broken all her own resolutions and betrayed her parents' trust. Now she has an agonizing decision to make which will affect all their lives. Amid all the turmoil and heartbreak, there is only one person who seems to understand what Cass is going through—the last person in the world that Cass would have chosen as a friend, the yobbish bully, James Derwent.

But James has problems of his own, and when these reach a crisis can Cass help him as he had helped her? And will she be in time . . . ?

Starlight City

ISBN 0 19 275041 0

'Where?' I asked. 'Where will you go?'

'The City,' she said.

'The City! Have you got any idea what it's like there? You won't last five minutes.'

It is the year 2050. When Kari's mother brings home a weird old woman she finds wandering in the road, Kari is appalled. What could have possessed her mother to pick up a scruffy old Misfit—or even a Drifter?

But Kari soon realizes there is more to Rachel than she first thought. There is something about her—her soft voice, her gentle aura, her love of music—which wins Kari over. So when the police arrive, looking for Rachel, and take her away for questioning, Kari decides she must go to the City and look for her, not realizing that this is just the beginning of an adventure that will change her life . . .

Winner of the South Lanarkshire Book Award

'A convincing twenty-first century world.'

Books for Keeps

The Shadow of August

ISBN 0 19 271595 X

'Mattie, you say your mum must have had a good reason to lie to you. Well, you're right, she did.'

When Mattie's mother dies, Mattie begins to discover that a lot of the things her mother had told her about her childhood weren't true after all. And the more Mattie tries to unravel her past, the more mysteries appear. Why had her mother never told her about the house in Cornwall? Why had she never met her grandparents? And who were the two figures who always seemed to be hovering on the edge of her life—just out of reach?

Eventually, Mattie feels that her whole existence is one big lie and that she can't be certain of anything.

'A convincing read—both plot and characters hold the reader's attention.'
   Books for Keeps

'A first-class mystery—a junior Ruth Rendell.'
   The Observer

'A gripping mystery.'
   The Times

The Night After Tomorrow
ISBN 0 19 275108 5

January . . . the wolf month . . . wolf-monath . . .

Jess felt she had been broken to pieces. Nothing worked for her any more. So it was good to get away and find some space with her aunt in the country.

But the country wasn't quite as peaceful as she thought it would be. In the forest there were strange noises and movements. When Jess was in bed, there was the sense of someone or something outside, watching, waiting for her. On the farms, the cattle and sheep were being slaughtered by a savage creature—the forest beast they called it.

And then there was Luc, who seemed to belong to the wild, with his hypnotic amber-coloured eyes and long hair. Why was he so interested in the forest beast? Why had no one ever seen his mother? And what was it that could only be done the night after tomorrow?

Winner of the Angus Book Award

'The ingredients of classic horror in this well-crafted and sensitive tale.'
> *Books for Keeps*

'This is a good, strong novel.'
> *School Librarian*

Charlie on the Spot

ISBN 0 19 271676 X

'Being almost fourteen's not all it's cracked up to be. Especially if you're a girl.'

Charlie has a lot of problems these days. Her mum is pregnant and has given up her job on the building site. Mum's partner, new-man Jed, is going to ante-natal classes and has started to suffer from morning sickness. And of course Mum has decided they're all going to move to the country.

Meanwhile, Mum has taken over the school pantomime which she thinks is sexist, cast Charlie as the policeperson, and showed Snow White how to defend herself from sexual harassment from the prince.

So, in the middle of all this, how is Charlie going to get the pair of spotted shoes she longs for? How is she going to become an actor? And above all, how is she going to get her first kiss from her alleged boy-friend, Gazza?

'An entertaining read.'
School Librarian

'Hilarious chaos!'
Books for Keeps

Other Oxford Children's Fiction

Warlands   Rachel Anderson

ISBN 0 19 271817 7

Once upon a time, quite a long time ago, in a beautiful faraway city where scarlet-flowering trees grew along wide streets, and where tropical sunsets reddened the evening skies, a small child was lying in the gutter . . .

When Amy goes to stay with her grandmother, she begs her to tell her stories about how Uncle Ho came to live with the family. Ho was a Vietnamese orphan, born amongst the bombings and terror of war, and the nightmares in his head are always with him.

No one really knows the true story of Ho's early life before he came to the family, but Amy's grandmother tells her the same stories she told Ho because, as her granny says, 'everyone needs to know the story of their life, even if it has to be invented.' And although the stories, like all good stories, start with 'Once upon a time,' Amy has to wait to find out if they will end with 'And they all lived happily ever after' . . .

Vixen's Haunt   Frankie Calvert

ISBN 0 19 271807 X

This was the last night she had of being a child. Tomorrow, another thing would begin.

It is Vixen's thirteenth birthday morning when her mother turns up unexpectedly. Vixen lives quite happily and calmly with her father. Her mother constantly travels the world, and Vixen very rarely sees her. This time, however, the surprise visit is only the beginning. It starts up a chain of events which lead Vixen to the most amazing discoveries.

Vixen has always loved foxes. When she was little she used to think she really was a fox. And all through her birthday summer, Vixen is haunted by the past, hunted by possible danger. But this time she can't run away.

Dark Thread   Pauline Chandler

ISBN 0 19 271761 8

'I thought I saw someone,' Kate murmured, shaking her head. She wondered if she was going mad.
'This place is full of ghosts,' the woman said, lightly.

Kate knows the mill well. She and her mother had an exhibition of their weaving there. Before.

But that was a different life, before the accident. And now Kate knows that she just can't cope any more.

But when she suddenly finds herself back in another world that is strange and familiar all at the same time, Kate finds that she has no choice. She has to keep going, to survive, and to protect the other people in her new family. This new way of life is exhausting and unrelenting. And in the background there is always the mill, with the machines that never stop, the work which never ends, and the dangerous power that drives it.

A Handful of Magic   Stephen Elboz

ISBN 0 19 271836 3

Suddenly Henry seemed to buckle at the knees. He let out a gasp of horror and his eyes jerked fully open. And snatching desperately at the air he slowly tipped backwards into the werewolves' den.

Kit, son of the Queen's witch doctor, takes his best friend, Prince Henry, on a night time adventure to see the werewolves at the Tower of London. Henry falls into the den and is bitten, causing a rift between the Queen and Kit's father. The Queen sends for Stafford Sparks, the Royal Superintendent of Scientific Progress, to cure Henry, declaring that magic is dead and that electricity is the power of the future.

Kit is sent to live with his Aunt Pearl in her weird home in the tower of St Paul's cathedral, but he is determined to save Henry from the clutches of Stafford Sparks and his electric shock treatments and prove that magic is still alive. But Kit's attempts to help his friend lead him into terrible danger in the tunnels under London, danger which even magic may not be able to overcome.

A Far Away Place   Harriet Graham

ISBN 0 19 271838 X

Coming closer, he could see that Josie was half out of the window with excitement . . . But she should never have got into the car at all. She knew the rules . . . Then he was level with the car and peering at the figure behind the wheel.

'Hello, Sean,' said his father.

At first, Sean doesn't see anything wrong with going for a burger with his father, even if it's not his regular day for visiting. But when the meal stretches to a weekend on a boat, and they end up in France, Sean begins to wonder if his father is telling him the truth. Why won't he let Sean phone his mother? And who is Isabella, the Spanish girl his father has brought with him? Sean starts to wonder if he and his sister, Josie, will ever see their mother and their friends again . . .

Daggers   Roger J. Green

ISBN 0 19 271828 2

'I was responsible for the death of a man once. I know I was. People would say I murdered him. I know I did. I killed him . . . His name was Edward. And I killed him.'

When Caroline reluctantly goes to see her Great-Aunt Clara in the old people's home, she is unprepared for the revelations that follow. Surely her aunt must be rambling; under the influence of all the medicines she is taking for the illnesses that have landed her in the home? How could her boring old aunt, who had spent all her life as a librarian, possibly have killed anyone?

But her aunt's confession seems to help Caroline in her own struggles to come to terms with her feelings for her parents. Maybe the key to her own animosity towards her father lies in the past and the family history her father is so keen to keep secret?

Facing the Dark   Michael Harrison

ISBN 0 19 271801 0

Everything had changed the moment I opened the door to the two men. It was worse, somehow, that I had been the one to let them in, the one who ended our family life.

Simon's father has been accused of the murder of a rival cab driver and Simon faces a life branded as the son of a murderer. Then he meets Charley, grieving for her dead father, the murder victim, and they determine to find out the real story behind the murder. Together they can face up to the danger which surrounds them, and bring back some hope for the future.

The Stones are Hatching   Geraldine McCaughrean

ISBN 0 19 271797 9

'You are the one,' he said. 'You must go. You must stop the Worm waking. You must save us.'

Phelim was the only one, they said, the only one who could save the world from the Hatchlings of the Stoor Worm. The Stoor Worm, who had been asleep for aeons, was beginning to waken. The dreadful sounds of war had roused it, and now its Hatchlings were abroad, terrorizing the people who had forgotten all about them, forgotten all the ancient magics.

But how could Phelim, who was only a boy, after all, save the world from all these dreadful monsters? And where could he find the Maiden, the Fool, and the Horse who were supposed to help him? As Phelim leaves his home and sets out on his quest, the words ring in his ears: 'You are the one. To stop the Worm waking. To do what must be done.'

Vicious Circle   Helena Pielichaty
ISBN 0 19 271775 8

'Why haven't we got any money? We've never got any money. Why can't we be like other people and have fish and chips when we fancy?'

Ten-year-old Louisa May and her mother Georgette are two of the 'have-nots', shuttling between ever-seedier bed and breakfast accommodation. To help cope with this way of life they play elaborate fantasy games, pretending to be the characters in the romantic fiction that Georgette borrows from the library in every town they move to.

When they arrive at the Cliff Top Villas Hotel in a run-down seaside resort and Georgette falls ill, it looks as if the fantasy will have to end. But Louisa May enlists the help of Joanna, another hotel resident, and together they determine to find out the truth behind Georgette's 'let's pretend' existence. Maybe this way there will be a chance for them to break out of the vicious circle and become 'haves' at last . . .

The Bold Enchanter   Weem Whitaker
ISBN 0 19 271759 6

'Ah, my dear,' answered the Enchanter with a thin smile, 'dreams can be very deceptive, you know.'

The Bold Enchanter is the one behind all the mischief. When the spells on Earth go wrong, and the wrong kind of magic is unleashed, Tom and Eleanor are the only ones who can save the kingdom. The Queen's wish for Magic and Mystery brought much more than she bargained for, and now someone has to sort it out. But that means many adventures and, somehow, Tom and Eleanor have to find their way to the moon.

The moon, of course, really is made of cheese—Edam, Stilton, every kind of cheese that you can think of. They have to cross the moon cheesescape of boiling Fondue and craggy Cheddar to face the Bold Enchanter in his own castle. Will they win? And what will it all be like when they get home again?